TAKEN BY THE CAPO

A DARK MAFIA REVENGE ROMANCE

TAKEN SERIES: THE LUCCHESE FAMILY
BOOK TWO

CHARMAINE LOUISE SHELTON

CONTENTS

AUTHOR'S NOTE

Dear Reader,

Taken by the Capo is a dark mafia romance intended for 18+ mature readers only.

If you love possessive, dominant Alpha males, forced proximity, mafia danger, surprise baby tropes, and a heroine who finds her strength even when trapped, then welcome to *La Famiglia*.

If you need soft and safe? This isn't that book.

Want it. Take it. And I want the trembling bella onstage.

Marcello

I live by the Lucchese family motto. And by my Taran Tactical Glocks. A mafia prince and the youngest born son of the Mafia Boss, nothing gets in the way of what I want. My father raised a ruthless assassin known as *The Hammer,* and I live up to my name. A dangerous man in a dark world.

Then Gala Zhukova steps onto the auction stage. An angel wrapped in gossamer. Her innocent light flickers in my darkness. No one can stop me from taking her. Not even my family's worse enemy—the Bratva who own my angel. And I'll burn the world down to keep her.

Gala

Raised in a house of horrors by a father who commits atrocious acts, I'm the next one torn from my sisters and sold to the burly men. My life goes from bad to worse. Then Marcello Lucchese takes me, and my world will never be the same. But my vow of revenge continues.

Will this brutal man help me or harm me further? And how can I fall in love with a monster?

Their spicy dark mafia revenge romance is a full-length standalone available in the Taken Series: The Lucchese Family. The interconnecting novels feature sexy as sin anti-heroes and the women who make their stony hearts beat. Get a glimpse of their dynamism in other books.

Anthem: "Melt With You" by Modern English
https://www.youtube.com/watch?v=LuN6gs0AJls

Content Warnings:

- 18+ mature readers
- Profanity
- Murder
- Violence
- Physical and mental abuse
- Sexual assault

- Incest
- Human trafficking
- Female auction
- Kidnapping

Visit CharmaineLouiseBooks.com

CHAPTER 1

ive Years Ago
Messina, Sicily
Marcello — 21

"Oh, I won't take your pussy cherry. But I will pop that ass of yours, *bella*. Your future husband will never know his fiancée isn't a virgin."

Giada Lombardi shivers as my warm breath skitters over the shell of her ear. Lips trail open-mouthed kisses down her neck to the juncture of her shoulder, where my teeth nip the sensitive flesh. A moan slips from her parted lips as she shudders against the wall pinned between my forearms.

I smirk at her reaction.

Niccolò Lombardi would have my balls if he knew my intentions for his seventeen-year-old eldest daughter, already promised to another man. The highest-ranking capo of my family's organization—*La Cosa Nostra*—Lombardi runs his slice of the pie and crew of soldiers with an iron fist.

But he's no match for mine—Marcello *The Hammer* Lucchese, third-born son of Vincenzo the Boss.

I live by our family's motto, *Want It. Take it.* And by my Taran Tactical Glocks.

A made man since my first kill to mark my thirteenth birthday. Nothing comes between me and what I want. Even as a child, I took whatever the fuck I wanted from others. If they refused, I hammered them. First with the toy car I wanted, then with my fists. They gave willingly or crying.

And Giada Lombardi will give crying my name as I pound my cock in her virgin ass.

My erection punches against the zipper of my bespoke tuxedo trousers. I grind my well-endowed junk against her pussy as my fingers tighten around her throat and one hip. My dick throbs as she gasps for air. Her pink, manicured fingernails claw at mine.

I lick up her throat to her slack mouth. The tip of my tongue rims her glossy lips. She moans while heavy lids lower over bright blue eyes. My tongue dives in. It sweeps the wet warmth to tangle with her tongue as she gives willingly.

Good girl.

Better to give me what I want than for me to take it.

Not that I need to take from women. Oh, no.

They drop to their knees or spread their legs for the baby face killer. The contrast of my soulful mink brown eyes and clean-shaven face with my reputation as a ruthless assassin makes their pussies wetter than the Ionian Sea off the coast of Sicily. I could drown a blissful death as I eat their pussies. Whores, socialites, mafia princesses all succumb to my mystique.

And Giada falls the hardest.

Her knees wobble as I kiss her breathless. Soft mewls escape her mouth. Hips gyrate as she meets the grinding of my pelvis. Yeah, she's ready.

I spin her around to face the wall. I can't help but to grind my cock against her round ass, driving her hip bones against the silk wallpaper. A good foot shorter than my six feet, four inches, I bend my knees to align her ass with my groin. Braced by my muscular thighs, I thrust up, lifting her to the balls of her feet in the high heels.

My hands place her palms against the wall as I press my front to her back. She moans and pushes her ass against me. Warm breath comes out in pants while her eyes squeeze shut. I can hear the thoughts as they race through her mind.

So good.

My father will kill me!

Oh, God, Marcello!

I snicker and nip at her nape. She squeaks.

"Keep your hands on the wall," I order as I press mine

on top of them. "Do not move unless I tell you. Understand, *bella*?"

She nods. Then yelps and her eyes pop open as my palm connects with her ass through the evening gown. She cranes her neck to look at me. I bunch her dress around her waist and pull her hips back.

"Wha—"

"Words, *bella*. I will have your words."

Her eyes flutter closed as I pepper her ass exposed by a skimpy thong with a flurry of spanks. The corners of my mouth quirk up and nostrils flare as I watch her creamy skin bloom a rosy pink.

"Use. Your. Words."

I punctuate each word with a spank that jiggles her reddened butt cheeks.

"I—I—I understand!" She wails, face flushed like her ass.

"Good girl."

I slide the tip of my middle finger along the inside of her thong, down to her pussy lips. The silk comes away soaked.

Giada likes it rough. Naughty girl.

She gasps and struggles to close her legs when my finger rims her slick pussy lips and slips inside to the second knuckle.

"No!"

"No?" I ask as my finger slides in and out of her tight pussy, eased by her natural lubricant.

"Y—You said you wouldn't touch me there. You said my butt, Marcello."

My wicked chuckle makes her tremble. Then she moans as I increase the pace of the thrusts.

"I never said I wouldn't touch your pussy, *bella*. And I am a man of my word."

Her pussy walls quiver around my thick finger. My ring finger flicks her engorged clit, and she goes off like a rocket.

Pussy grips my finger. Juices gush into my palm. Mouth forms a perfect O as a throaty moan pours from between her parted lips. My thighs press against the backs of hers to keep her from collapsing to the floor as her entire body convulses.

Damn. Has no man set her off?

What a dumb fuck her fiancé must be.

My fingers continue their magic, drawing out her orgasm until she's still. A satisfied smirk spreads across my face as I lean into her ear and nip the delicate lobe.

"You're ready to take my cock in your ass now, *bella*—"

I jerk away and rise to my full height as the sounds of shouts and screams infiltrate the room. My gaze swivels to the door of the meeting room next to the grand ballroom in the hotel owned by my family. The clicking of high heels on marble and the heavier thudding of men's shoes as guests run past the door adds to the unexpected chaos.

What the fuck could happen at my older sister Gemma's engagement party to Giada's brother Renzo?

I don't waste time figuring it out. Instead, I grab Giada by the arm and pull her to the conference table. Dragging a chair away, I push her forward.

"Hide under the table until your family comes for you. Do not leave this room. Understand?"

This time, I don't demand her words. She nods as her wide eyes flick between me and the door where the hysteria increases. Without hesitation, she scampers under the table. I roll the chair back in place before I rush for the door. I slam the lights off and crack the door open.

Automatically, my hands go to my Taran Tactical Glocks in the holsters beneath my tuxedo jacket and click the safeties off. I whip them out as I step from the room. The door closes behind me with a soft snick. Guests race past me, fleeing the ballroom. I run to it.

"Fuck you, Ludovico! Fuck you too, Luca! And to hell with you, Flavio! You think you're tough shit as the Boss' sons? It's time for the Lucchese rule to end! It may not be me. But someone will take you out! End your fucking line for good!"

Renzo glares through blackened eyes as he kneels before my older brothers. Bloody spittle lands on Ludovico's shiny patent leather dress shoes. His face remains impassive as he holds one of his Heckler & Kochs to Renzo's forehead.

Around them—also on their knees—Niccolò, his two

younger sons, and his top soldiers glare with eyes full of hatred. Luca, Flavio, and some of our soldiers train their guns on them.

In search of my parents and sisters, Gemma and Allegra, my gaze roves over those remaining in the ballroom. The Lombardi women—except from Giada—huddle in a corner surrounded by more of our soldiers. Other capos and their soldiers stand to the side. But no sign of the rest of my family. My heart lurches in my chest as I run to my brothers' sides.

I aim my guns at Niccolò. He spits at my feet. I don't flinch. But my fingers itch on the twin triggers.

"It won't be you."

The crack of the gun as it discharges a bullet into Renzo's skull reverberates around the ballroom. His head snaps back at the force as a hole appears between his eyes. Another crack signals the shot to his heart. Women scream.

I don't have to look at Ludovico to know the process. Our father taught us to shoot between the eyes and in the heart to ensure the kill.

Renzo Lombardi is no more.

His father roars at the death of his heir and rises to one foot.

I shoot his kneecap.

He screams in agony and falls to his side, covering the blown joint with his hands. Blood oozes past his trousers and between his fingers.

"Do not kill him, Marcello."

Luca's calm command stills my trigger fingers.

"End the others."

Without hesitation, Flavio, our soldiers, and I kill them. The room erupts in gunfire, screams, and shouts. A single gunshot aimed at the ceiling silences the ballroom. All eyes shift to Luca.

The eldest of the Lucchese siblings at twenty-five and the identical twin to Ludovico stalks towards Niccolò. My brother moves with the grace of a predator as he focuses his sharp brown eyes on the fallen capo. Their eyes meet. Neither cowers.

"You dare to kill our father while our mother rides in the car with him on their way to your son's engagement party to our sister? You break the code of no harm to women and to children. So you can take over what my family has run for generations? The Lucchese's rule *La Cosa Nostra*."

My heart skips a beat.

However, years of trainings—including beatings by my father's hands—prevent me from displaying any reaction and damn sure no emotion. I sense the eyes of the other capos and their soldiers on my brothers and me. I remain still with my guns at the ready.

"You dare to speak to me like I'm someone beneath you, boy?! You're still shooting blanks. I don't give a fuck who you think you are."

Ludovico and Flavio flank Luca. Niccolò gives them a scathing look and spits at their feet.

"Marcello, bring Giada from wherever you were fucking her."

The son of another capo utters a string of Italian curses. But he shuts his mouth with a quickness when a soldier faces him.

"You filthy animal! If you laid a fucking hand on my daughter—"

Ludovico knocks the words from Niccolò's mouth with the butt of his gun. A glob of blood mixed with broken teeth lands on the floor. Wordlessly, Ludo steps back.

I stride from the ballroom and return with a frightened Giada gripped by the elbow.

"Father!"

She jerks. But I hold her fast and drag her to Luca.

"My father taught us an eye for an eye—"

"No! Please! Please, Luca! I beg you! Do not kill my daughter! We know nothing!"

The Lombardi matriarch's cries ring out in the ballroom. She pleads while we stare impassively.

She cries, and my mother is dead.

I give zero fucks. Kill the bitch.

Interestingly, Giada's fiancé remains silent. I flick my gaze from him back to Niccolò. He rises to his knees. A grimace crosses his face at the pressure on the shattered joint. He clasps his hands together and lowers his gaze in supplication.

"Luca, Giada's mother is correct. They know nothing

of my plan to overtake your father. The women are innocent—"

"As was my mother."

Niccolò flinches at the deadly tone. But he continues to beg.

"Please, Luca, let them live. You killed my sons and my soldiers involved. Kill me now. But have mercy on Giada. Please."

Silence descends.

Giada and the other women cry softly.

Two gunshots ring out.

The body crumples to the ground.

Screams and shouts fill the air.

CHAPTER 2

resent — Russia
Gala

"IRINA."

My stomach drops as our father Borislav rises from the table and calls to my oldest sister. The already silent and cold kitchen plunges into a soundless, frozen tomb. Even Borya and Yeva—her three-year-old son and her two-year-old daughter—know better than to speak when their father calls for Irina. No one says a word as he stalks from the kitchen and she follows him meekly without a glance at us.

Not until their bedroom door closes do we breathe.

I jump from my chair and clatter the forks as I collect them from the table. As the next oldest sister remaining at the farm, I attempt to cloak the sound of the bedsprings as he rapes his own daughter.

Tasha—my youngest sister by seven years—gathers Borya and Yeva from their chairs. She leads them to the bedroom they share to shield them from their grandfather-cum-father's atrocious act. I nod as she glances over her shoulder at me. She returns the nod with solemn eyes.

Since our mother Nina died as she gave birth to Tasha, our father turned to Irina to warm his bed and ignored baby Tasha. But from the time she understood words, he cursed her for the death of his wife. Tasha stopped speaking at three years old. Eight years passed.

Syuzanna—two years younger than me—flinches when Irina's muffled cry reaches the kitchen. She does her best to remain quiet through the regular assaults. But we know our father is rough with her. The bruises around her neck and on her arms and her hips prove he's the monster we know.

I shake my head at Syuzanna.

She hurries to put on her threadbare coat. With a glance at the kitchen entry, she leaves the room to put the meager bits of remaining dinner in the cold storage shed outside. The freezing winter temperatures will keep them edible for breakfast.

I wash the dishes in the thawed block of ice in the sink. Syuzanna returns and dries them. My mind flashes back to our mother—our saving grace.

Twenty years younger than our father, she was a

teacher in the village several miles away from our remote farm. Unfortunately for her, she met our father at the weekly market where he sells meat from his pigs. He charmed her with his good looks and smooth words. She married him despite her parents' disapproval. They disowned her and never spoke to her again.

My fondest memories of our mother were of the times she taught us our lessons. She was determined to educate us despite the chances of us ever leaving this godforsaken area of Russia are nil. However, each morning she taught reading comprehension followed by the English language. The afternoons focused on math and history. When we scored high on our tests, she drew stars and smiley faces on the pages, then hung them on the special wall in the hallway.

Our father was loving and kind. He'd praise us when he returned from the market or from the fields. Sometimes he brought our mother trinkets he traded with others. She'd make a show of the handmade necklaces as though the finest diamonds adorned the chains. He beamed at her, and they disappeared into their bedroom.

Then our lives went to hell.

He wanted a son to carry his name.

Our mother delivered three girls, followed by a still-born son. Our father turned to drinking. He became abusive. Curses yelled at Irina when she didn't shut the front door and let the cold air inside. Katya—my second oldest sister—forced to stand in the rain when she tracked mud in the living room. A slap to my face when I dropped the pig slop outside of their pens. Worse of all, he beat out mother and called her a lazy whore when she didn't prepare his dinner to his liking.

Our happy home turned into a living nightmare.

But he still wanted a son.

For years, he bred our mother, no different from the sows. She gave birth to Syuzanna and another stillborn son. Our father cursed her even as her health deteriorated. Gone was our cheerful mother with the shining dove gray eyes—so like mine. Only a fragile husk of a woman remained. Her skin paler than her waist-length ash blonde hair, again another trait of hers I bear. But he didn't stop.

His hopes of a son died with Tasha. Our father took one look at the baby girl and left the house cursing.

Irina chose her name since it means birthday. I helped Katya to clean our mother and our baby sister. Papa returned drunk and covered in dirt. He took our mother bound in a sheet and buried her in the yard. We watched as he shoveled dirt over her lifeless body. That night, he came for Irina. She was sixteen.

When she screamed from our parents' bedroom, Katya and I raced from the one we shared. We banged on their door. The angry muffled voice of our father sounded before Irina's teary one. She told us she was fine and begged for us to go back to sleep.

We waited outside the door and heard the bedsprings creak like they did when our mother was in the room.

Our father's grunts and groans blended with them. Irina's soft cries broke my heart.

Katya snatched my hand as I raised it to bang on the door and covered my mouth. She dragged me to our bedroom and closed the door. Silently, she moved me to the bed, where she told me to sleep.

That was the first night I dreamed of killing my father.

Four years later, and I still want him dead.

His sick obsession with Irina continues. But last year, he stooped to a new low.

Every year, giant, scary men arrive at the village. They demand tribute from the poor families and give them little money in exchange. Their trade? The untouched eighteen-year-old girls. We only learned of their visits when our father came home last year and told Katya to pack a bag. I dared to question him. He cuffed me upside the head. The world tilted before I slammed into the wall. Katya scurried to do his bidding.

An hour later, a windowless, black van drove into our yard. Three burly men piled out while the driver remained behind the wheel. Our father rushed from the house and greeted them. They glanced over as he gestured behind him to where my sisters and I huddled at the window.

Terror gripped us when our father called for Katya. It was worse than when he called for Irina. We held tight to Katya. He charged inside and dragged her screaming and crying from our grips. A backhand to the face sent

Syuzanna reeling. I ran after him as he yanked Katya through the front door.

The men eyed her appreciatively and expressed their approval. Like our mother and me, Katya has the same light hair and eyes, tall, and naturally slim from years of little to eat. One man took her by the arm and pushed her toward the back of the van, where another man opened the door. Her cries silenced as they slammed the door shut.

I shouted and ran forward, only for our father to stick out his arm. It caught me at the throat, and I fell to my knees in the dirt. Even as I gasped for breath, I cried Katy's name.

Our father thanked the men for the bag of money and watched as they climbed into the van and drove off. I fell to my face and cried until no tears remained. Syuzanna and Tasha helped me to my feet and half carried me to the house. We passed our father as he left.

Hours later, he returned singing loudly as the front door slammed shut. Irina jumped from my bed where she stayed when he wasn't around. Her wide eyes stared at the door. On cue, he called for her. Dejectedly, she left the bedroom. Fresh tears fell from my eyes as Syuzanna, Tasha, and I held Borya and Yeva close.

Now, it's my turn.

During dinner, our father told me to pack a bag. My sisters peeked at me. The fork halfway to my mouth hung suspended as I realized the implication of his words. The burly men were coming for me. I'd never return, just as we've never seen Katya again. The fork lowered to my plate. Bile rose in my throat. The thought of escaping leaped into my mind. Then our father spoke.

"Unless you want Syuzanna to go in your place, you will pack your bag after you wash the dishes. Tomorrow morning, you will leave. Be thankful I gave you time to say goodbye to your siblings."

He finished his dinner and called for Irina.

Now, as I glance at the few ragged clothes I own, Syuzanna tries to console me. Tasha watches. Her eyes shine with tears. I must be strong for them.

"Listen to me," I say as I face my younger sisters as they sit on the bed while Borya and Yeva play on the floor. "Syuzanna, you are the eldest now. Take care of Tasha. Don't leave everything for Irina to do. She has enough with Papa."

"Y—Yes, Gala."

"Tasha, be brave. Watch after the little ones."

She nods as trails of tears glisten on her pale cheeks. Her brown eyes flick from me to Borya and Yeva. As though sensing the tension, they toddle to me and wrap their arms around my legs. As my belly roils, I swallow back a sob and crouch, then draw them into my arms. I bury my face in the black hair they inherited from our father. Closing my eyes, I inhale their soap scent to imprint it on my mind. I rise with them in my arms and place them on the bed.

"Be good, *malen'kiye*," I whisper as I ruffle their hair,

then glance at my sisters. "I will always think of you. I love you."

They burst into tears. My bravado fades as I collapse on the bed and cry.

The next morning, I refuse to shed a tear as a burly man bustles me in the back of another windowless black van. Five girls with hands bound sit on benches lined along the side walls. Eyes rimmed in red, stare at me.

"Don't cause trouble, or you'll be sorry," the largest man threatens as he sits me on a bench and binds my hands with plastic. He lowers his massive frame on the end and punches the roof twice. The van shifts into gear and lurches forward.

I close my eyes and say a prayer to watch over my siblings and to give me the strength to handle whatever the men plan. I keep them closed as I turn my thoughts inward to block the sound of the girls crying.

Tingling at the back of my neck alerts me to someone's gaze on me. My eyes open to find the man staring at me. He licks his lips. I avert my eyes. But the movement of his hand draws my attention.

Thick, muscular thighs spread wide. His hand strokes his penis as it sticks out of his pants.

My head jerks towards the rear door as a gasp slips past my lips.

He chuckles darkly.

"This may be the first cock you've seen. But it won't be the last. Get used to it, *shlyukha*."

CHAPTER 3

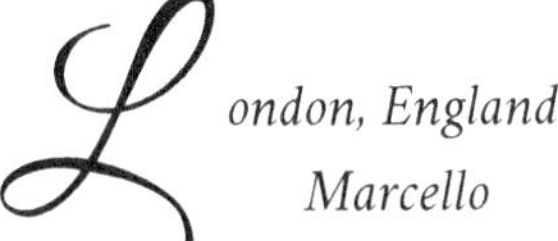
ondon, England
Marcello

"Ladies and gentlemen, the auction begins in five minutes. Bids recognized by paddles and through phone calls via representatives. The opening bid is fifty-thousand pounds. We offer three lots this evening. Only one per bidder. Select wisely. You reviewed the photographs. Now, prepare for them to dazzle you with their beauty. Ready to satisfy your every carnal pleasure and kink. Good luck, ladies and gentlemen."

"Here we go, Marcello. I promise you, this bunch will prove why we should partner with the Bratva if only for a cut of the profits. Look at all these buyers. Lined up to get some virgin Russian pussy…"

Tommaso Russo—our capo for the UK—drones on.

Luca has no interest in human trafficking. Once he replaced our father as Boss, Luca began the divestment of our family's less than savory involvements. Aside from a few high-end men's clubs where the women willingly work—including this one—he sold the other establishments.

Our primary focus is as arms dealers. We provide the largest assortment in the world for top-quality weaponry. Individuals and organizations seek us out for pistols to missiles. It's so lucrative, our revenue increased despite the loss of the other involvements.

But with our enemy the Bratva making inroads with these new auctions, I came to witness one. They supply the girls. We provide the club. Profits split—in our favor, naturally.

I'll form an opinion and present it to Luca and Ludovico, our underboss. Flavio, our consigliere, will offer his impartial advice. Perhaps a partnership where our enemy bows to us will provide an opportunity for me to prove to my brothers I'm as powerful and feared as they are.

My gaze roams around the private room of the luxury members-only club in Mayfair. Hidden in plain sight in the center of London's ritzy neighborhood. Twenty women and men in designer dresses and custom-tailored suits drip in diamonds and flash pricey watches on their wrists. Magnums of Champagne flow as the bidders await the first lot. Eyes gleam as they flip through the glossy brochure. Eagerly, they lean forward when the lights dim on the stage. The auctioneer announces the first lot.

Four teenage girls dressed in skimpy lingerie step from behind the curtain. They move across the stage on fuck-me stilettos. Wobbly legs barely carry them to the center. As if signaled, they turn and face the bidders. The girls squint in the light's glare. It blinds them but high-lights their hauntingly beautiful faces.

I've fucked plenty of gorgeous women. These do nothing for me. I view them as potential commodities in the chess game of power—nothing more. But they impress the bidders as their paddles rise in quick succession and representatives raise theirs for the phone participants.

The prices soar with the second lot. By the third, the auctioneer's oily voice describes the upcoming girls as the most sought after of the night, sure to delight their new owners.

"Let's see what these broads have that makes them so special."

Tommaso leans forward. His words draw me from my musings.

I glance at Faustino and Donatello Romano. The imposing and serious brothers serve as my right-hand men and would take a bullet for me. Faustino cocks an eyebrow. Donatello shrugs. Neither impressed so far. My gaze returns to the stage.

Instead of the girls appearing in a group, the auctioneer calls to them one at a time. The first two get scooped up after bidding wars. When the auctioneer introduces the last girl, he all but rubs his hands together as his eyes glint in the light.

"Gala, an ethereal beauty. Ash blonde hair with fathomless dove gray eyes and unblemished alabaster skin. Five feet, eight inches of luscious breasts and long, toned legs. An untouched beauty ready to blossom for a lucky winner. Gala, come."

He raises his hand towards the side stage. A hush descends on the room where only two bidders remain. I watch them lean forward as eager as Tommaso. I fight the urge to roll my eyes. Finish this shit already.

But then she appears. An angel in a sheer tulle white babydoll and G-string.

She stumbles forward, then catches her balance on the impossibly high stilettos. The curtain of her waist-length hair covers her face. She brushes it behind her shoulders as she stands trembling in the center of the stage. Eyes wide as her pale, oval-shaped face flushes crimson when the auctioneer orders her to turn in a slow circle.

Plump dusky pink nipples pucker behind the demi cups. Succulent full tits overflow the tops. Her narrow waist leads to hips not too wide and not too narrow, perfect to grip when fucking. Legs for days to wrap around my ears as I feast on her pussy or locked around my hips as I piston in and out of her cunt. An ass my sizable hands can cup and ripe for a spanking followed by a sound fucking makes me bite back a groan.

I can smell her innocence. My cock hardens painfully.

Without hesitation, I rise from the barstool and stalk towards the angel with the body of sin.

"Ah, sir, if you care to bid, kindly use your paddle."

Eyes focused on the angel, I ignore the auctioneer and hop onto the stage. Her eyes widen as she steps back. My eyes narrow. Hers flick to the auctioneer then return to mine. Tommaso calls my name. He's ignored as I bend and put my shoulder against her flat belly. I rise and hop off the stage.

"Hey! You can't just take her! I want to bid."

Ignored.

Russian voices rise behind me.

Three of the Bratva bratok shove to their feet, paddles clattering to the floor. The largest of them, a shaved-headed bull of a man Faustino will later identify as Petrov—one of Sobol's London crew—takes two steps forward before Faustino's Glock finds the center of his forehead. The other two freeze.

Sobol. I file the name. We'll have a conversation about that later.

Faustino and Donatello flank me with their guns pointed at the Bratva bratok. The rest of my soldiers follow suit. Tommaso takes point. We move through the club and out the side door. My SUV waits. Tommaso and Faustino check the alley while Donatello covers my rear. They signal the all clear and open the doors.

I shift the angel to my arms and slide into the back. Tommaso shuts the door and taps the roof. The SUV pulls off as Faustino and Donatello jump in and close their doors. They don't look at me. They know me by now.

But the angel doesn't.

"W-who are you?"

"The beast to your beauty."

Want it. Take it. And I want the trembling *bella* onstage.

So, I took her.

CHAPTER 4

$\mathcal{M}$*arcello*

THE MAYFAIR PENTHOUSE rises twenty-seven floors above the street and the street is already a different world from that club—the low thrum of traffic, the amber wash of London at midnight through floor-to-ceiling glass, the particular hush that only obscene money can buy. I have stood in this room a hundred times. Tonight, with a trembling Russian angel planted in the center of my white marble floor, it feels like somewhere I have never been before.

She doesn't look at the view. Smart girl.

Her eyes move the way mine do when I enter an unfamiliar room—not admiring, assessing. Exit to the left. Kitchen to the right. Two men visible, Faustino near the bar, Donatello at the hallway. Her gaze clocks each of them, measures them, files them. Then it returns to me, steady as a compass needle, and I feel it like a thumb pressed to the center of my chest.

Dio. She is something.

Ash blonde hair—waist-length, tangled from being thrown over my shoulder like cargo—falls in curtains around a face that belongs on the altar of a church, not in a Mayfair auction room or in the sights of every man with a paddle and a sick appetite. Oval face. Cheekbones like carved ivory. Lips pressed together so firmly they've gone pale at the edges. And those eyes—dove gray, still and deep and full of a calculation so precise it makes my cock stir and my jaw set in equal measure.

Terrified. She's not showing it, and I respect that more than I can say.

The demi-cup babydoll and G-string are still what she wears. The stilettos make her nearly my height, which is an unexpected problem because it puts her mouth at exactly the wrong level for a man trying to think clearly.

My suit jacket is off my shoulders before the thought fully forms. I cross to her in four strides and drop it around her shoulders.

She flinches at the sudden proximity, that pale throat working as she swallows. Then she pulls the lapels together with both hands. Her knuckles are white.

"Thank you."

Her English is excellent, the accent soft and precise,

the kind that comes from books and a careful teacher rather than television. Something about that detail lodges in me like a splinter. I file it and pull out my phone.

He materializes at my shoulder—six-four of calm lethality, mahogany hair, obsidian eyes already reading the situation beneath the shadow of a jaw that hasn't seen a razor in three days. The Romano brothers are built from the same mold: broad, olive-skinned, the kind of men a room notices and then reconsiders.

Donatello is the sharper edge of the two—imposing where Faustino is watchful, a withering stare where his brother offers a raised eyebrow. My right hand. My brother in everything but blood. He has been at my side since before I could shave, and he has a gift for knowing what I need before I ask for it.

Almost before I ask for it.

A pause. Barely half a second, but I know Donatello well enough to read the entire sentence he doesn't speak out loud.

Another pause. Then he nods once and steps away, phone to his ear, and I catch the quiet warmth that moves through his voice when the line connects—the particular softening that only happens when he speaks to Paolina.

It used to irritate me how thoroughly that woman rearranged him. Standing here watching this pale girl grip my jacket lapels like armor, I find I have slightly less room to be irritated about it than I used to.

Faustino pours two glasses of water and sets them on the coffee table without being asked. His expression communicates nothing except that it has already assessed everything and found it acceptable. My left hand. Steady as stone, sharp as a blade, lucky as his name promises. The three of us have been the point of every operation for four years. We don't need words for the fundamentals.

The angel—Gala—watches Donatello move to the window with his phone and Faustino retreat to the kitchen, and I see her recalibrating. She expected something else. Chaos, perhaps. Cruelty. The kind of room where men shout and grab and take what they want with their hands, because that is the only kind of room she has ever been inside.

I want to know who built that expectation into her. And I want to break their hands.

The thought is immediate and disproportionate, and I am a man who does not do disproportionate. I set it aside.

Donatello returns with a folded stack of clothes—one of my shirts, a pair of Gemma's sweatpants left here from her last London visit, thick socks. He sets them on the arm of the sofa with the wordless precision of a man who grew up in service to this family and has long since understood that service has nothing to do with submission. He catches my eye and tips his head toward the hallway.

I grunt.

Donatello retreats.

Gala watches this exchange. When I turn back to her, those gray eyes are slightly less flat than before. There's a thread of confusion in them, like a woman who walked into a room expecting one mathematics and found another.

Her chin lifts. A fraction of an inch—a tell so small most men would miss it.

I don't miss tells. 'What's that about' is what the lift of that chin says, and we both know she's right, and we both know I'm also right, because the first thing a girl on an auction stage understands is hierarchy.

She takes the clothes. She doesn't thank me this time.

I don't want her to. Instead, I point to the powder room.

She returns. The shirt—charcoal, my monogram at the cuff, sized for my chest—swamps her to mid-thigh. My sweatpants bunched at her waist, tied in a knot to keep them up. The stilettos are gone, her feet bare on the marble, and without those four inches of heel she is smaller than she looked on the stage, softer, younger, and so heartbreakingly out of place in this penthouse that something in my ribcage does something I choose not to examine.

The stage makeup is gone, and what's underneath it is extraordinary—not the performance of beauty the auction dressed her in but the real thing, unadorned. Clear skin. The faintest shadows under her eyes. A lower lip with a healed split at the corner, old enough to have faded to a thin white line but recent enough to tell me it happened within the last year.

Someone hit her. Someone hit her mouth.

My molars press together. I keep my face blank.

Faustino laid the coffee table with food—Donatello called ahead to the restaurant two blocks over, the one that owes the family a significant favor and doesn't ask questions. Roast chicken. Bread. Roasted vegetables. Simple. Real. Food that feeds a person rather than impresses one.

She stops at the edge of the rug and looks at the table. Something flickers across her face. It's there and gone in under a second, but I catch it. Not greed. Not appetite. Something more complicated than either. A wariness, as if abundance is the setup for something worse.

Christ. What did they do to her?

She glances at me. Then at the food. Then she sits on the edge of the sofa—not settling, perching, ready to move—and she begins to eat. Slowly. Controlled. Small bites, deliberate chewing, like someone rationing a resource that has always been scarce. She eats the way people eat who have learned someone may take the plate away.

I drink my espresso and don't watch her. Or I watch her the way I watch everything I need to understand— peripherally, steadily, building a picture.

When she's eaten half of what's on the plate, she stops and sets down her fork. Not because she's finished, but because she's decided half is sufficient; taking more than half is dangerous.

I want to tell her she can eat all of it. Let her know there's more in the kitchen. I don't, because she will read it as pity and close back up like a fist, and the small opening she has allowed is worth more to me right now than her being fed.

She absorbs this. Her eyes do that cataloguing thing again—reading me, reading the room, reading the quality of the silence and what it means. She isn't a woman who takes statements on faith. She wants the architecture of certainty, not just certainty itself.

Good. That will keep her alive.

"Who are you? Why did you take me?"

The question lands flat and direct, with no tremor in it. Those dove-gray eyes are steady on mine.

I could say no. It would be the simple answer. But she's too intelligent for simple answers, and lying to a woman who reads rooms the way she does will cost me more than the truth.

"Marcello Lucchese. I took you because I wanted you. That's reason enough. You were in the wrong place, owned by the wrong men who can no longer touch you. Now you're not. You're here. With me. And you're not leaving."

A long pause. The city hums twenty-seven floors below. Somewhere in the penthouse, Donatello speaks in low Italian on his phone, and from the softness of his voice, I know it's Paolina again.

Gala blinks. She expected me to argue, to override, to deploy the weight of my name and my organization and my fifty kilos of tactical advantage. Instead, I gave her acknowledgment, and she doesn't know what to do with it. The wariness flickers back. This time aimed not at the food or the room but at me specifically.

Smart girl. I am the most dangerous thing in this apartment.

I look at her for a moment. The honest answer is that I don't know yet. That something happened when she walked out from behind that curtain, trembling and defiant in equal measure, and my body decided before my mind had the paperwork ready. That the thought of another man's paddle going up for her made something in me go very cold and very certain. Want it. Take it. has been the family's motto my entire life and tonight, for the first time, it felt like more than a transaction.

I don't say any of that.

The guest room is at the end of the hall—king bed, white linen, blackout curtains, its own bathroom. Understated and expensive, the way all of my spaces are. I push the door open and stand back.

She moves past me into the room, and I catch her scent—something underneath the auction's perfume, something that's purely her. Clean. Faintly warm. My hand tightens on the doorframe.

She turns to look at me, standing in the middle of the room in my shirt and her bare feet, and for one unguarded second something crosses her face that isn't calculation or survival or wariness. Something younger. Something that might, in a different life, in a safer world, have been relief.

Then it's gone. Her chin lifts.

"Thank you," she says. Precise. Neutral. The two words cost her nothing because she's decided they cost her nothing.

"Tomorrow morning we leave for Sicily."

She flinches.

"I can't leave without finding my sister," she starts, then rushes on in my silence. "The Bratva have them too. They've stolen girls from my village." Her eyes darken to steel before she spits out, "My father sold us to them. And I'll make him pay."

My eyebrow rises at her hatred, and inwardly I vow to get her revenge.

"I will handle it," I respond as I pull the door shut.

Four seconds later, from the other side of the wood, I hear the snick of the lock turning.

I don't move for a moment. My hand still rests on the door handle, and the apartment is quiet around me, and Donatello's voice has gone silent from wherever he was talking to Paolina, and the city breathes twenty-seven floors below.

She locked it.

Good.

The corner of my mouth pulls. Just barely. I push off the door and move back toward the living room, rolling my shirtsleeves down, and I don't examine the fact that I want, more than I have wanted anything in recent memory, to be on the other side of that door.

Donatello is at the bar, pouring two glasses of Barolo. He holds one out as I approach. We drink in silence for a moment, the way men who have known each other since boyhood can.

A pause. He turns his glass, looking at the wine, not at me. "You've never asked for Paolina before," he says. "For any of them."

He doesn't push it. That's what I value most about Donatello Romano—he knows the precise moment when a man needs space around a thought. He raises his glass instead. I raise mine.

We drink.

I refill my glass and take it to the window, looking out at the city—the orange-lit canyons of Mayfair, the distant black ribbon of the Thames, the indifferent glitter of a world that doesn't know or care what happened in a private auction room tonight. My phone buzzes. A Bratva number—the third time in the last two hours. I look at it. I set it face down on the glass.

Faustino appears at my shoulder. His voice is quiet, factual. The tone he uses when the information is significant and he wants me to have it without theater.

"They registered the number to a shell company tied to Yuri Sobol's London operation. He runs the Bratva's European auction network. Answers to someone above him, whose name we don't have yet." A pause. "But we have Sobol."

Sobol. His name lands, and I file it with the same cold efficiency I file all intelligence. The man who put her on that stage. The man whose crew Petrov belongs to. One name at the end of a thread I intend to pull until the entire network unravels.

They want her back.

They are welcome to come and try.

Somewhere down the hall, behind a locked door, an ash-blonde girl in my shirt is lying in a bed that isn't a barn floor or a trafficker's van bench or a stage in a Mayfair club. The thought of what put her on that stage in the first place—the bruise on her wrist, the healed split on her lip, the way she ate like someone rationing a resource that has always been scarce—coils in my chest like a wire pulled tight.

She asked me why her.

I don't know yet. But I am going to find out.

I pick up my phone and dial Donatello. He answers on the first ring—he always answers on the first ring, as if sleep is something that happens to other people.

A beat of silence. Then, as quiet and certain as everything Donatello does, "Consider it done."

I end the call. Set the phone on the glass ledge. Finish my wine.

Down the hall, the lock holds.

For now, let it hold. She has earned the night.

Tomorrow, we fly to Sicily. And then we begin.

ala

THE BED IS the first thing I notice when I wake up .

Not the unfamiliar ceiling, not the gray London light pressing through the gap in the blackout curtains, not the distant sound of a city I have never seen in daylight. The bed. The mattress is so deep and so clean that for one disoriented moment I think I am still dreaming—still in the place my mind builds when it needs somewhere safe, the imaginary room I have retreated to since I was fourteen years old, the one with the door that locks and the window that faces something other than a pig field.

Then the events of last night reassemble themselves

in the correct order, and the dream dissolves. I'm fully awake.

Marcello Lucchese's penthouse. London. Mayfair.

My eyes move to the room's other details with the methodical sweep I learned not from any school but from living in a house where danger could come through any door at any hour: a single window, curtained, no fire escape visible through the gap. One interior door, the bathroom. No connecting door to another room. The furniture is sparse and expensive. Pieces too heavy for me to move, which means none of it is useful as a barricade. But some of it could serve as a weapon in the right circumstances.

Old habits.

I sit up and push my hair back from my face. The shirt I slept in—his shirt, charcoal cotton, the monogram ML at the left cuff—is warm and absurdly soft and smells of something dark and clean that I refuse to think about. The sweatpants still knotted at my waist. My bare feet find the floor, cool marble, real beneath my soles. I press them flat and breathe.

The lock I turned with my own hand still engaged—I check it before I check anything else, a reflex so practiced it happens before thought. Engaged. Good.

Alive. Unhurt. Fed, even, which is more than I can say for most mornings of the last four years.

What does he want from me?

The question circling since the moment he lifted me off that stage—not with cruelty, not with the casual brutality of the men in the van, but with a kind of absolute certainty that was more frightening than either.

He carried me like a decision he had already made. He gave me a locked room and food with no conditions attached and the name of the man who built the cage around me, spoken simply: I am Marcello Lucchese. As though that explained everything.

Perhaps it is.

I learned a long time ago that the most dangerous men do not need to shout. My father shouted. The men in the van shouted. The auctioneer, with his oily voice and glossy brochure, spoke in the tone of a man who has never needed to raise his voice because the room was already arranged for his bidding. Marcello Lucchese does not speak loudly. He speaks once, and the room rearranges itself.

I need to understand him before he understands me. Whoever gets there first has the advantage.

He stocked the bathroom the way I imagine hotels in cities I have never visited are stocked—bottles lined up in a row, shampoo and conditioner and something labeled body wash in a font that implies it costs more than my father's monthly earnings from the pig market.

I stand in front of the mirror for a moment before I turn the shower on, looking at the face that stared back at me from that stage last night. Oval. Pale. The shadows under eyes that have not slept properly for longer than I can calculate. The old scar at the corner of my lip, the one I tell myself I have stopped noticing.

He noticed it. I saw his jaw tighten.

The observation sits in me, neither comforting nor alarming. A data point. I file it and turn on the shower.

The water is hot.

This is the thing I am not prepared for—not the luxury of the products lined up on the shelf, not the size of the shower enclosure or the weight of the white towel, or even the absence of a mildew smell. The hot water.

Back home, we heated water by dragging a pot to the wood stove and waiting, and in winter the waiting was longer. The pot was never large enough. We learned to wash fast and without complaint because complaints changed nothing and used energy we could not spare.

Here the water arrives hot from the wall without asking, steady and inexhaustible. The temperature is adjustable with one hand.

I stand under it and let the water hit my shoulders and the back of my neck as I think. Syuzanna. Tasha. Irina. Borya and Yeva, who have never had hot water from a wall tap in their lives.

I will come back for you. I will find a way.

The tears fall before I can stop them, soundless, lost immediately in the steam and the water, and I let them come for exactly sixty seconds—I count—because grief without a limit is a luxury I cannot afford. At sixty, I press both palms flat against the tile and breathe until I am steady. Then I wash my hair with the expensive shampoo that smells of something floral and European, and I do not cry again, and when I step out and wrap myself in the white towel, I am composed.

Composed is the only armor I have ever had that no one can take away.

The penthouse is different in daylight. Larger, somehow, the floor-to-ceiling windows turning London's gray morning sky into something almost beautiful. The city spread out below in layers of rooftops, spires, and the River Thames—a pewter ribbon in the distance. I stand at the glass for a moment, my reflection ghosted over the cityscape, and I think how I have been nowhere this high. The tallest thing near our farm was the pine forest on the ridge, and that was not tall so much as dense, pressing down rather than lifting.

Here, everything lifts.

The kitchen is to the right. I catalogued it last night, but daylight changes rooms. Marble countertops. A coffee machine that requires separate education to operate. And behind the counter, already doing something efficient with cups and a small pot, stands a man Marcello called Faustino.

He looks up when he hears my silent footfall. My presence is enough to alert him. His eyes—dark, careful, reading me with precision—move across my face once and then return to the cups. He's built like Donatello but differently arranged: the same height, olive skin and dark coloring, the same broad-shouldered frame that speaks of a man who could break things effortlessly and chooses, in this moment, not to. Where Donatello's stillness is imposing, Faustino's is measured. Watchful rather than waiting. The difference between a predator at rest and a predator at work.

Brothers. Not twins—different jaw, different set to the eyes. But the same blood is obvious.

He sets a cup of coffee on the counter and steps back without a word. The gesture is neutral, not servile, not threatening. Simply, here is coffee. It's yours if you want it.

I want it.

The first sip is strong enough to make my eyes water slightly, rich and dark in a way that has nothing to do with the instant granules dissolved in lukewarm water that passed for coffee at home. I wrap both hands around the cup and let the warmth travel up my arms as I think, with a clarity that surprises me: I could think clearly here, if I am careful. There are resources in this place— money, men, reach. Marcello Lucchese said the Bratva cannot touch me while his name stands between us. If that is true, even temporarily, then I am safer now than I have been in a while.

Use it. Think. What do you need, and how do you get it?

What I need is Katya. And Irina and Syuzanna and Tasha and the children. And Borislav Zhukova dead in the dirt of his own yard.

One thing at a time.

Marcello appears from the hallway at the exact moment I finish the coffee, as though the apartment has alerted him. Dark suit, freshly pressed, jaw clean-shaven

—the baby face that I watched last night. He is devastatingly put together for a man who looks like he's stayed up all night.

Mink brown eyes find mine across the kitchen counter. Something moves in them—there and gone, a flicker of something that is not the cold assessment I expected—before his expression settles back into that particular neutrality that tells me nothing and everything at once.

"You slept," he states. Not a question.

"Yes," I set the cup down. "You didn't."

The corner of his mouth twitches. Not quite a smile. "No."

He crosses to the machine, does something to it with practiced efficiency that produces an espresso in under thirty seconds. He leans against the counter with the cup, watching me with the same sidelong attention he used last night—the kind that is not quite looking directly, which means it misses nothing.

"We fly to Sicily in two hours."

"You said this morning."

"I say it again so it's not a surprise."

This consideration is so unexpected that I simply look at him for a moment. He doesn't explain it, doesn't underscore it, doesn't seem to notice that he's just done something no man in my life has ever done—warned me of something in advance so I could prepare.

Careful. That is not kindness. That is strategy.

Isn't it?

Before I can decide, the sound of rotor blades cuts through the double-glazed quiet of the penthouse windows. Marcello's eyes flick to the ceiling—not in alarm, but in recognition—and something in his posture shifts. A fraction of a degree. The neutrality warms, marginally, in a way I would have missed if I were not watching him as carefully as he is watching me.

"Paolina," he says. To Faustino, not to me. Though his eyes stay on mine.

Faustino moves toward the elevator without being asked. The rotor sound grows and then changes pitch—landing, I realize. On the roof. There is a helipad on the roof of this building, and apparently, this is simply a normal thing that happens.

Who are these people?

The elevator opens four minutes later.

The woman who steps out is not what I expected, and I realize, cataloguing my own assumptions, that I have been braced for another version of the auction—another version of beauty deployed as currency, all performance and surface. What I get instead is a woman in dark jeans and an oversized cream sweater, raven hair loose and waist-length, moss green eyes that take in the room with a single sweep and land on me with an expression so immediately, genuinely warm that my chest does something I am not prepared for.

She looks at me the way my mother used to look at us after a hard day on the farm—like I matter. Like she is relieved to see me upright.

Behind her, Donatello steps out of the elevator with a small, dark-haired child balanced on his forearm, as if she weighs nothing, which she nearly does. The child's eyes are enormous and serious as she clutches a worn stuffed rabbit by one ear with the absolute conviction of someone who has never considered that the rabbit might have somewhere else to be.

Donatello and Marcello exchange a look over the tops of everyone's heads—the look that contains an entire conversation compressed into half a second—and then Donatello moves to the kitchen with his daughter and his brother and leaves Paolina standing three feet from me.

She doesn't extend her hand. She tilts her head slightly, her eyes read my face with a frankness that is not intrusive. It is the frankness of someone who has been exactly where I am standing and wants me to know they survived it.

"Gala," she says. Her English carries the lilt of Italian beneath it, warm and unhurried. "I'm Paolina. I came from the island." A slight pause. "He called Donatello at midnight and said bring me. So." Her chin tips toward Marcello—not possessively, not with resentment, with the particular exasperation of a woman who has long since made peace with the fact that the men in her orbit do not ask, they simply act. "Here I am with Cosima."

I don't know what to say. The honest answer is that I don't know why she is here, what role Marcello expects her to play, whether this is surveillance in a softer form. The honest answer is that I want to sit down with this woman and her stuffed-rabbit child and not move for a week. Happy to be around family once again.

I reveal none of these thoughts. "Thank you for coming."

Her expression does something complicated—a flash of understanding so precise it makes my throat tighten. She nods once.

Then she says, quietly, so only I hear it, "I know what this is. I know what it feels like when someone takes you out of one world and drops you in another one and doesn't explain the rules. I'm not here to watch you." A beat. "I'm here because I wanted someone to do this for me, and no one did."

Oh.

I look at her for a long moment. She looks back without flinching. Behind us, from the kitchen, Cosima announces something in rapid Italian that includes the word *coniglio*—rabbit—and Donatello's low voice responds with patience that sounds thoroughly practiced.

Marcello appears in the kitchen doorway. His eyes move from Paolina to me and back, and whatever he reads in the distance between us makes that almost-smile pull at the corner of his mouth again.

"We leave in ninety minutes," he says. "There's breakfast."

Paolina touches my arm—light, brief, asking nothing—and tips her head toward the kitchen. I follow her. Cosima, upon seeing a new face, fixes me with the solemn stare of a child conducting a serious evaluation, then extends the rabbit toward me with both hands. An offering. Or a test.

I take the rabbit carefully in both hands and hold it with the gravity it deserves.

Cosima nods. Apparently, I have passed.

For the first time since the van, I almost smile.

The flight to Sicily is three hours long.

Paolina sits beside me and talks, not about anything that matters, not at first. The easy surface conversation of a woman who understands that one cannot rush trust. She tells me about her Mediterranean private island—the light there in the mornings, the way Cosima has learned to say the names of every fish Donatello brings in from the boat, the lemon trees that grow almost to the water's edge.

She talks the way my mother used to talk during lessons—understanding the actual subject is not the subject. That what she is actually doing is making a space I can choose to enter.

I watch Sicily appear beneath the plane—golden-brown and ancient, pushing up out of the blue Mediterranean like something that has always been there and always will be, indifferent to the history that has washed over it. The light here differs from Russia's. Thicker. As though the air itself is made of something warmer.

Marcello is three rows ahead of me, talking low with Faustino and Donatello, his dark head bent over something on a phone. He hasn't looked back at me since we boarded. He's giving me the space—consciously, deliberately—to exist on this plane without his attention pressing on me. The observation makes something complicated move through my chest.

Stop noticing him.

Stop noticing the things he does that are not what you expected.

Paolina leans slightly toward me. Her voice drops. "He's not what you think," she murmurs. Not reading my mind—reading my face, the way women who have survived difficult things learn to read each other.

"What do I think?" I ask.

She considers.

"That he took you because he wanted something. That there are conditions on the food and the safety and the room with the lock."

Her eyes are steady on mine.

"There aren't. I know, because Donatello took me too, and I spent three months waiting for the conditions to arrive. They didn't." She pauses. "That doesn't mean it isn't complicated. It is. These men are"—she searches for the word—"a lot." A small, wry curve to her mouth. "But they don't take without giving back. That's the thing no one tells you."

I look at her for a long moment. The plane banks slightly, Sicily tilting in the window, the sea flashing gold where the sun hit it.

"He said he would find my sister," I say. The words come out quieter than I intend.

Paolina doesn't flinch or soften or fill the statement with reassurances I haven't asked for. She simply nods. "Then he will," she says. "That's not a line with Marcello. When he says something, he means it. And when he means it—" she glances toward the front of the plane, toward the dark head bent over the phone, and something in her expression is both fond and faintly awed— "nothing in the world gets in his way."

I file this. I file everything.

But underneath the filing, underneath the cataloguing and the survival math and the careful measurement of every door and every exit and every man in every room —underneath all of it, something very small and very cautious lifts its head.

Something that might, in a different life, in a safer world, be called hope.

I press it back down. Not yet. Not until I understand what this place is and what it costs and whether the man who brought me here is worth the trust I can feel, against all my better judgment, beginning to form.

Sicily rises to meet us. The wheels find the runway. Marcello is on his feet before the plane stops moving, phone to his ear, already thinking three moves ahead of this moment. I can see it in the set of his shoulders, the particular tension of a man who does not experience stillness as rest but as inefficiency.

Paolina stands and lifts Cosima, who immediately demands coniglio, and Donatello produces the rabbit from somewhere without breaking his conversation with

Faustino, which tells me everything about the daily choreography of that family.

Marcello pauses at the front of the plane and looks back. Not at the group—at me. Directly. Eyes find mine across the length of the cabin, and he holds them for exactly two seconds, and in those two seconds, I read something I am not supposed to read, something he is not aware he is showing. He is checking. Making sure I am all right. Making sure the landing wasn't frightening, or the flight, or the proximity to all these large, armed, complicated men.

He looks away before I can decide what to do with that.

Don't. Don't do that. Don't let him be someone who checks up on you.

Too late.

Sicily smells of citrus and sun-warmed stone and something wild underneath that I have no word for. When I step off the plane, the heat lands on my skin like a hand.

I stand at the top of the stairs for one breath and let myself feel it—the warmth, the light, the blue of the sky above an island I have never imagined being on. The world is bigger than the farm. The world is bigger than the van and the auction room and the cold Russian dark.

I will save my sisters. I will burn my father's world to the ground. And then I will figure out what this is.

Below, black SUVs wait.

Marcello is already moving toward them, the men

fanning around him like a tide, the operation of his life continuing without pause. He uses his hands when he speaks, I notice—a quick, illustrative gesture as he says something to Faustino, the Italian quick and liquid between them.

Paolina appears at my shoulder. "Ready?" she asks.

No. Yes. The two answers exist in me simultaneously, and I am not sure which one is the truth.

"Yes," I tell her.

She nods.

We walk down the stairs together, into the Sicilian light, and the heat wraps around me like something I didn't know I needed, and below, without looking back, Marcello opens the door of the Cullinan and waits.

 *arcello*

THE GULFSTREAM BANKS over the Ionian Sea on approach to Catania and from the window the water is the color of hammered bronze in the afternoon light, and Sicily rises from it the way it always does—like something that preceded the world and will outlast it. I've flown this approach hundreds of times. Today, for reasons I refuse to examine, I look back down the cabin to check that she is seeing it.

She is. Eyes stare out the window, something in her face that she hasn't locked away in time—a kind of stilled wonder. The expression of someone who has received nothing beautiful without a price attached and is bracing for the invoice. Paolina says something low beside her.

Gala's expression closes again, but the wonder leaves a ghost.

She has been nowhere.

Someone kept her somewhere small on purpose. I want to find that someone and take them apart slowly.

The fury is clean and specific. I set it aside. Fury without information is wasteful. Faustino is already running the investigation. I will have what I need soon enough. For now, land, drive, install her at the villa, deal with Luca.

The SUVs wait at the edge of the tarmac, black and low in the Catanian heat—four vehicles, eight soldiers, the welcome that is both escort and statement. My men know how to communicate significance without a word being spoken. The Bratva have been making noise since London. Let them hear this noise in return.

Gala comes down the stairs with Paolina at her shoulder and stops at the bottom, and the Sicilian heat hits her the way it hits everyone who arrives from the gray north—like a physical thing, a hand on the chest. She breathes it in. One deliberate breath, eyes closing for half a second, and I watch something in her posture shift: the shoulders drop one degree. Just one. But on a woman who has been holding herself at full tension since the moment I put her over my shoulder in a Mayfair club, one degree is significant.

Good. Let the island do some of the work.

I open the Cullinan's rear door and wait. She sees it, glances at me, and something passes across her face—not gratitude, not submission, but a kind of measured acknowledgment. She gets in without being told twice. Paolina follows with Cosima, who has apparently decided that Gala is now her primary person of interest and is attempting to share the rabbit with her again.

Donatello slides into the front without a word. Faustino takes the vehicle behind us. I get in, pull the door, and the convoy moves.

The drive from Catania to the family compound at Lucca Sicula takes an hour through the interior of the island—past the volcanic black rock and the citrus groves and the ancient dry-stone walls that divide the hillside terraces, past the small towns with their Baroque churches and their old men outside bars playing cards in the shade. Sicily doesn't perform for visitors. It simply is, and you either understand it or you don't.

Gala watches all of it from the window with that same careful attention she turns on everything. Her reflection in the glass shows me what she's hiding from the room—a jaw that has slowly unclenched. Eyes that have gone a fraction softer.

Sicily is doing its job.

Cosima falls asleep on Paolina's lap somewhere past Enna, the rabbit tucked under her chin. The vehicle goes quiet in the particular, comfortable way of people who do not need to fill silence with noise.

Donatello's eyes find mine in the rearview mirror once. I give him nothing. He gives me the same. Between us, thirty years of knowing each other handle the entire conversation without a syllable.

The villa appears above the tree line as we climb the last approach road—the compound walls first, pale limestone against the blue sky, and then the main house, low and spreading and rooted in the hillside as though it grew there. Three generations of Luccheses have lived within those walls. We buried my parents in the family chapel at the east end of the property. I don't look in its direction when we pass it. I never do.

Gemma is on the front steps.

My older sister, at twenty-eight, is the most dangerous member of this family in the way that the family least expects—not with guns or strategy but with a social intelligence so precise it operates like a scalpel. She reads people the way I read threats—instantly, completely, without apparent effort. She takes one look at Gala stepping out of the Cullinan and, in the two-second window before anyone speaks, I see her assess, conclude, and decide.

She moves past me entirely.

"Gala." She extends both hands, not to shake—but to take Gala's hands in hers, warm and direct. "I'm Gemma. Welcome." Her accented English is fluent, and her voice carries the specific warmth of a woman who has decided you matter before she knows your name. "Come inside. The heat is impossible, and the lemon granita is cold."

Gala blinks. Expectation braced her for something else—for the household to mirror its owner, cool and contained and waiting to be explained to. Instead, she has Gemma, who explains nothing and welcomes everything. I watch her look at my sister for one long moment.

Then, quietly, she lets Gemma lead her inside.

Gemma. Good.

I catch my sister's eye over Gala's shoulder as they go through the door. Gemma's expression is the one she used to make when we were children and I had done something that required managing—half-exasperated, half-approving, entirely aware of what it means that I have brought a woman to this house for the first time in my adult life.

Her arched eyebrow says, we will discuss this.

My expression says, not yet.

Luca calls before I've made it through the front door.

I take the call in the study—the room that was our father's, that still smells faintly of the Havanas Vincenzo Lucchese favored and the particular leather of the chair behind the desk. Luca's voice comes through the line at the temperature it reaches when he is containing something significant—precise, level, each word placed with the care of a man who knows the weight of them.

"Tell me you're at the villa."

"Just arrived."

"And the girl?"

"Settled."

A silence. I know this silence. It's the one Luca uses to let the weight of a situation establish itself before he applies pressure. He learned it from our father. I learned the same silence from the same source, which means we are both aware of what it means and it fool neither of us.

"The Bratva have been on every channel since London," he says. "Three of our cargo holds in Palermo flagged for inspection this morning. Coincidental, of course."

"Of course."

"The Mayfair club is asking questions through Tommaso. The auctioneer—"

"The auctioneer should ask himself whether he wants to continue to have a larynx," I say. "He put a girl on a stage who did not belong there. The Bratva brought her to London. I removed her. The sequence is simple."

Another silence. Luca's kind.

"First Donatello takes someone he shouldn't, now you. You went to that auction to observe," he says. "To form an opinion and report back. That was the assignment, Marcello."

"I formed my opinion. The Bratva are using our club's infrastructure to traffic women and calling it a partnership. My opinion is that we don't partner with people who do that. My opinion is that the girl comes home with me." I pause. "I'll write it up if you need it formally."

The silence this time is shorter.

"She stays a week." His voice is final. How Luca's voice is always final. The tone of a man who's been Boss since twenty-five and has never needed to repeat himself. "Then she goes. Wherever she chooses to go. We find a solution for the Bratva situation that does not involve a liability living in our family compound indefinitely."

"No."

The word lands in the silence and sits there. Faustino, who's appeared in the doorway to deliver something, goes still.

"Excuse me?" Luca says.

"Gala stays. She's not a liability, and she's not a week's problem to be solved. She stays."

I keep my voice level, which costs me something, because the thought of Gala being loaded into a car and driven away from this compound in seven days produces a response in me that is neither level nor professional.

"I'll handle the Bratva, Tommaso, and the cargo holds in Palermo. That is what I do, *fratello*. Trust me to do it."

The longest silence yet.

I wait it out.

Outside the study window, the olive trees at the edge of the courtyard move in the afternoon wind. Somewhere inside the villa, Gemma's voice drifts she's talking to Gala, the warm, unhurried cadence of someone introducing a place to a person they've already decided belongs there.

"Flavio wants to speak to you," Luca says finally. "He'll be in Catania by Friday. Dinner at the villa. Be there." A pause. "And Marcello, whatever this is, keep it controlled. The family cannot afford sentiment as a strategy."

The line ends.

Faustino raises one eyebrow. He sets the folder he's

carrying on the corner of the desk—the preliminary investigator's report. He taps it once with two fingers and leaves the room without speaking.

He's added a second sheet to the front of the folder. A name at the top: Yuri Sobol. Beneath it: London-based, runs the Bratva's European auction and trafficking network, operating through three shell companies registered in Cyprus. Estimated seven years running this specific circuit. Answers to a Pakhan whose identity Faustino's network has not yet confirmed—recently inherited the organization, Moscow-based, believed to be in his early forties. The investigation is ongoing.

Sobol is the face. Someone above Sobol is the architect. I want both names on my desk before this is over. Not for the family—for the girl upstairs and her sister who got put on a London stage by the network this man runs.

This man. Worth his weight in gold and whatever the metal above gold is called.

The report is twelve pages long.

Borislav Zhukova, fifty-three. Pig farmer. Remote settlement in the Perm Krai region of Russia, two hundred kilometers from the nearest city of any size. No criminal record—in this part of Russia, what he does to his daughters does not produce a criminal record because no one in authority has noticed it or cared to. Father of six daughters, all born of one wife—Nina Zhukova, née Sorokina—who died delivering the youngest approximately eight years ago. The oldest daughter, Irina, currently twenty-two, has remained on the farm.

I read that sentence twice.

Currently, at the farm. With him.

The second daughter, Ekaterina—Katya—their father sold to traffickers approximately fourteen months ago. The investigator traced her to London, then Warsaw, then a last known location: a safe house in Warsaw run by Bratva-adjacent operatives. Three more daughters: Syuzanna, sixteen; the youngest, Natalya—Tasha— eleven, reported mute. And Gala, eighteen, second oldest after Irina, sold four weeks ago to clear a recurring debt the father carries with local traffickers who pass the women up the chain to the Bratva auction circuit.

The folder shakes. I realize it's my hands.

I set it on the desk. Flatten both palms against the leather surface. Breathe, slow and deliberate, the way Donatello's father taught me before a fight—from the diaphragm, not the chest, let the oxygen do the work before I make any decision. Our father taught us to suppress reactions entirely. Old man Romano taught us to process it first and then act. Between the two methods, Romano's produces fewer mistakes.

He sold her. Her own father sold her. And the sister before her. And there are three more still in that house.

The fury is not clean this time. It's dense and specific and personal in a way that has nothing to do with La Cosa Nostra or the Bratva or Luca's warning about sentiment as strategy.

A pig farmer in the Perm Krai region sold his daughters to clear a debt, and one of those daughters is currently in my villa eating Gemma's lemon granita and trying to decide whether to trust me, and she has been carrying this since she was fourteen years old.

I know now.

I pick up my phone. Dial.

Faustino answers on the first ring.

"Warsaw first," I say. "Katya Zhukova, the last known location, the safe house. Eyes on it by tomorrow morning. Quietly. No movement yet, just confirmation she's there."

"Already tasked," Faustino says. "Donatello has a contact in Warsaw who can confirm by tonight."

Of course he does.

"The farm in Russia. Layout—buildings, access roads, how many people on the property at any time. Everything." I pause. "The father stays alive until I say otherwise. He's not touched."

A beat of silence.

"Understood," Faustino says. Not asking why. Not asking what comes next. In eighteen years of working together, Faustino Romano has never once asked why.

I end the call. Sit for a moment in my father's chair in my father's study with the olive trees moving outside the window and the family chapel just visible at the far end of the property.

You built this empire so your children would be safe. You put us in this life so nothing could touch us.

And something touched you anyway.

The thought is familiar, and I put it back in its drawer. There is work to do.

I stand, button my jacket, and go to find Gala.

I find her in the garden off the east wing. Gemma's domain, the one with the lemon trees and the low stone wall where the view opens onto the valley below, and on a cloudless afternoon you can see the sea. Gemma has apparently installed her there with a glass of granita and then diplomatically disappeared, because Gala is alone, sitting on the wall with her bare feet on the warm stone, looking out at the valley with the expression of someone given too many things at once to process.

The light here in the late afternoon is the amber that painters come to Sicily to chase. It hits the ash blonde of her hair and turns it to something warmer, and the dove gray eyes, when she turns at the sound of my footsteps, catch it too. She looks different outside than she did in the penthouse. More real. Less like a woman bracing for impact and more like a woman who has briefly allowed herself to be somewhere.

I sit on the wall at a distance that is not intimate but not indifferent. She does not move away. We look at the valley for a moment.

"Your sister Gemma," she says. "She doesn't ask questions."

"No. She asks them later, privately, and already knows the answers. She just waits to confirm."

A momentary silence. Then, almost despite herself, the corner of Gala's mouth moves.

There it is. There's the smile she's been keeping locked up since London.

It's gone in a second. But I saw it.

"Tell me about your family," I say.

The stillness that moves through her is immediate. The particular freeze of someone asked a question they've been rehearsing an evasion for and are now being caught before the evasion is ready. Those gray eyes find mine. Read me. Look for the motive behind the question.

I wait. I have learned more patience in forty-eight hours than I have exercised in the previous twenty-six years.

She looks back at the valley. When she speaks, her Russian accent thickens on the edges of the words.

"My mother was a teacher," she says. "She taught us every morning. Reading, English, mathematics. She drew gold stars on our test pages and hung them on a wall in the hallway."

She stops.

"She died eight years ago," she continues. "Tasha—my youngest sister—was born, and our mother didn't survive it. Tasha never speaks. She hasn't spoken in eight years."

I do not speak. I keep my eyes on the valley and let her feel that I am listening without making the listening about me.

"My father became someone else after our mother

died. The someone else he became sold Katya. My second oldest sister." Her voice is flat. The flatness is not detachment. It's the specific tone of a person who has told themselves a story so many times that the telling has worn smooth. "That was fourteen months ago. I haven't seen her since." A pause. "I don't know if she's alive."

The last sentence costs her something. I can hear it in the fraction of a second before she says it, the breath she takes to steady herself.

"She's alive," I say.

Gala turns to look at me. Fast, sharp, those gray eyes cutting.

"How do you know?"

"Because I started looking," I tell her. "Donatello has a contact in Warsaw with eyes on a location by tonight."

The silence that follows is not the wary silence she's been keeping since London. It is a different kind— denser, more fragile. The silence of someone receiving information they didn't allow themselves to want, because wanting it was too dangerous.

Her throat works.

"You were looking for her before I said anything," she says. Not a question.

"Yes."

"Why?"

The honest answer is in the twelve-page report on my father's desk, and in the sound of my own hands shaking over it, and in the specific quality of the fury that has been burning in my chest since I read the word currently regarding Irina still at the farm. The honest answer is that she walked off that auction stage trembling and defiant, and something in me recognized something I cannot yet name.

I look at her for a moment.

"Because someone should have stopped this long before now," I respond.

Her eyes hold mine. Something passes through them —a wave of something vast and unguarded. The thing she has been locking away since the van and the stage and the penthouse and the flight, the thing that Paolina's kindness and Gemma's warmth and Cosima's rabbit have been quietly working at for twenty-four hours. It arrives all at once, and it hits her like the Sicilian heat hit her at the bottom of those stairs.

She doesn't cry loudly. The tears arrive without sound, tracking down those pale cheekbones, and she doesn't raise her hands to stop them because her hands are gripping the edge of the wall. She's holding on.

I don't reach for her. I sit still and let her have it. All of it, every tear, the van and the stage and the eight years of carrying this alone have owed her. Because she's earned it, and because the one thing I will not do is make this about me.

When the wave passes, she takes a breath. Both hands press flat against her face for a moment, then drop. Her spine returns to vertical. Her chin lifts.

Composed again. Armor back in place. But the armor is different now—less brittle. As though something inside it has shifted to make room for the fact she's not carrying this alone anymore.

I reach into my jacket and produce a handkerchief—linen, with my initials, which she finds as absurd as I expected her to. Her eyes flick to it, then to my face and back. This time the corner of her mouth moves for longer than a second.

"Of course you carry a handkerchief," she smirks.

"I'm Sicilian," I say. "We're prepared."

She takes it. Presses it briefly to her face. Returns it with the precise care of someone raised to handle other people's things carefully, because replacing them was never possible. I put it back in my pocket without comment.

We sit for a while in the amber light, looking at the valley. Below, the citrus groves step down the hillside toward the flat plain and the distant glimmer of the sea. The air smells of lemons and warm stone. The evening comes in slow and golden, the way Sicilian evenings do—as if the day is not ending so much as deepening.

"Your other sisters," I say eventually. "Irina. Syuzanna. Tasha."

Her jaw tightens.

"Still at the farm," she tells me. "Irina stayed because she had nowhere to go. Because our father—"

She stops. The accent thickens. She's deciding how much to tell me, measuring the risk of it, and I do not push.

She tells me enough. Not everything. The surface of

it. The shape. Enough for me to understand what the farm is and what it costs, and what needs to happen.

My hands are still in my lap.

He dies. That's already decided. The only question is when and how, and who gets to do it.

And I already know the answer to who.

"We'll get them out," I say. "All of them. Irina. Syuzanna. Tasha. The children. Katya too. We find her in Warsaw, and we bring her here." I hold her gaze. "This is not a maybe, Gala. This is a plan."

She looks at me for a long time.

The light is going now. The amber deepening toward rose. Her face in this light is the most complicated, beautiful thing I have ever looked at. The survivor's wariness, and the underneath of it, the woman who drew stars on test pages in her head and waited eight years for the world to be different.

"Why?" she asks again. The same question. Quieter this time.

This time I don't answer with a line about what should have been stopped. I look at her for one moment longer than is strictly professional.

"Because you are mine to protect," I say. "Even if you don't know it yet."

The words land between us, and she doesn't flinch from them the way I expected. She looks at them—considers them with those filing, measuring, survival-trained eyes. Something settles in her face that's not agreement but isn't rejection either.

The villa lights come on behind us, warm gold spilling from the windows. Somewhere inside, Cosima is announcing something loudly to Paolina, and Donatello's voice follows—patient, amused, the bass note of a man who has entirely rearranged his life around two people and found the arrangement suits him. From the kitchen comes the smell of whatever Gemma is making for dinner, something with herbs from the garden and the olive oil pressed from the trees at the compound's edge.

Gala turns back to the darkening valley. She doesn't tell me I'm wrong.

Good enough. For now, good enough.

I stand. Button my jacket. Look down at her—barefoot on the warm stone wall, the light leaving her hair.

"Dinner is at eight," I say. "You'll offend Gemma if you're not there."

"Would I actually offend Gemma, or would she just want me to think she is?"

"Both," I say. "Simultaneously. She's very skilled."

This time the corner of her mouth moves and stays Small. Private. Real.

I walk back inside before I do something inadvisable. Behind me the Sicilian evening finishes arriving, and the stars begin.

CHAPTER 7

ala

DAWN ARRIVES in Sicily differently than anywhere else I've been, which is nowhere and everywhere now. The light comes in pale gold before it warms. The birds begin before the light. By the time the sun clears the ridge behind the villa, the air already smells of the lemon trees and the dew on the stone walls and something else underneath, something ancient that has no name in Russian or in the English my mother taught me.

I've been awake for an hour. Not from fear—that is the first thing I notice. I woke because I'm not accustomed to silence, to the particular quality of a house where no one is coming through a door with harmful intent. My body doesn't know what to do with safe. It keeps checking.

Learn. Adapt. This is what survival looks like now—adjusting to the absence of danger as quickly as you adjusted to its presence.

The room they've given me is on the east side of the villa—my choice, I discovered, when Gemma showed me three options last night and simply waited while I walked through each doorway and assessed each window. She didn't ask why I needed to assess the windows. She just waited. The east room has two exits, a view of the courtyard, and a bathroom with a lock. I chose it in under a minute, and Gemma said only, *Good light in the mornings.*

She was right. The light is extraordinary.

I'm in the library when I hear him. Not footsteps—a presence, the shift in the air's quality that I've been cataloguing for a week now without meaning to. The specific atmospheric change that announces Marcello Lucchese before I see him. I don't look up from the Italian grammar book immediately. I make myself finish the sentence I was tracing with my finger: *il verbo essere*, the verb to be. To exist. To be present in a place.

Appropriate.

He leans in the doorway.

I can feel it. The weight of his attention, which differs from other men's attention in a way I have been trying to quantify since London. Other men's attention lands on you. His attention encompasses you. The way a room encompasses furniture. Ss though you're a thing he's already accounted for in the architecture of his thinking and is now simply checking against reality.

I look up.

He's in a white shirt this morning, sleeves already rolled to the elbow, the expensive watch at his wrist catching the early light. Dark hair, still damp from a shower. Clean-shaven, the baby face that the Mayfair room underestimated until the SUVs appeared at the side exit. Those mink brown eyes find mine and settle there with the comfort of something that has found its preferred location.

Stop noticing the details. You're gathering intelligence, not making an inventory of a man you—

Stop.

He pushes off the doorframe and comes to sit beside me on the reading bench without asking, the way he enters all spaces—as though the question of permission has already been answered. He leans forward and looks at the open page. His shoulder is an inch from mine. The space between us is warmer than the rest of the room.

"Il verbo essere," he says. His Italian is silk over stone —effortless, native, the accent of a man for whom this language is but breathed, not learned. He taps the page. "You're pronouncing the e too closed. In Sicilian Italian it opens more." He says it, "Essere." Then waits.

I repeat it.

His mouth moves—a slight correction at the corner, showing me the shape of the vowel without making it a lesson. I say it again. He nods.

His mouth is—

The verb. Focus on the verb.

"Why Italian?" he asks.

"Because I'm here," I say. "If I'm going to be here, I should understand it."

He's quiet for a moment. The morning light moves across the spines of the books on the shelves—old ones, some of them, the kind that get passed down rather than purchased. A family's reading life, accumulated across generations. My mother would have stood in this room and been unable to leave it.

Mama. I will hang so many stars for you. I will teach your grandchildren the way you taught me, and I will draw stars on every page.

The thought arrives with the grief attached, the way it always does—sudden and whole, a wave I can either drown in or ride. I ride it. I press my finger to the next word in the grammar book. *Avere*. To have.

Marcello watches me do this. He says nothing about what he sees on my face, and his not-saying-anything is so carefully chosen that it communicates more than speech would.

"Tell me about your family," he says. And something in his voice differs from the first night in the garden— softer. Not the commanding patience of a man waiting for intelligence, but the genuine question of someone who wants to know.

I consider the risk of it. I've been considering the risk of everything since I arrived—every meal, every kindness, every unlocked door. Paolina told me there are no conditions attached. Gemma welcomed me before she knew my name. Cosima offered me her rabbit. And Marcello, who could have taken everything from me on a London stage, gave me a locked door and a handkerchief and said, *because someone should have stopped this.*

He ordered the investigation before I told him anything. He was already looking for Katya.

I tell him about our mother. Not the performance of it, not the surface version I gave him in the garden—the real one. Nina Sorokina, who married a pig farmer against her parents' wishes and brought her books with her and taught us to read in a farmhouse kitchen and hung gold stars on the wall. Who made a feast of thin soup and called it rich. Who loved our father until he gave her no choice but to stop.

Marcello listens. He doesn't interrupt. Nor does he offer the reflexive reassurances that people use to manage their own discomfort with someone else's pain. He simply listens, his forearms on his knees, his eyes on the middle distance, receiving everything I say with the full weight of his attention.

When I stop, the library is quiet.

Then, without planning it, without the cost-benefit analysis I have been running on every word since London, I tell him about Irina.

Not all of it. Enough. The shape of it. The terrible simple shape of what our father has been doing since our mother died, and the way Irina carries it, and the way we all carry it for her, and the way I have dreamed of ending it since I was fourteen years old lying awake in the room next door listening to the bedsprings.

My voice stays level. I've told myself this story so many times that the telling has worn grooves, smooth and passable. But my hands—I look down and find them gripped together in my lap, the knuckles pale.

A warm weight settles over them. His hand, covering both of mine, not gripping—just present. Covering. Still.

I look at his hand on mine, and something in my chest does something I will not name. His thumb moves once across my knuckles—one pass, deliberate, acknowledging—and then stays still.

"He dies," Marcello says. Quiet. Certain. Not a question, not a threat, simply a fact being stated into the room. "When this is over. He dies."

I lift my eyes to his.

His eyes are steady on mine, and what I see in them is not the cold professionalism of a man arranging the logistics of a problem. It's something much more personal. Something that looks, if I'm reading it correctly, like fury on my behalf. Fury that has been sitting in him since before I told him any of this.

Marcello read the file. He already knew. He's been carrying this fury for me since the report arrived, and he said nothing, just sat with me in the garden, and let me decide when to speak.

The wave arrives again. This time it is not grief. It's something else. Something I have no Russian or English word for, something that lives in the space between relief and terror and the first fragile understanding that you are not alone.

The tears come before I can stop them. Not the silent ones from the shower or the garden—these shake me, just briefly, just once, before I pull them back.

His hand stays over mine. He doesn't move toward me, doesn't make it a rescue, just keeps his hand where it is and lets me feel what I feel without making it smaller.

When I'm done, I straighten.

His hand lifts from mine, allowing me back to myself.

He produces another handkerchief from his pocket.

I press it to my face. When I lower it, I find him watching me with that expression I'm still learning to read. The one that's not possessive or calculating, or performing tenderness. But something underneath all of those, something quiet and specific and aimed entirely at me.

"Keep it," he says, nodding at the handkerchief.

I almost laugh. The almost-laugh surprises me more than the tears did.

"I'll return it laundered," I say.

"I have thirty others," he says.

"Of course you do."

This time the almost-laugh becomes a real one—brief, quiet, escaping before I can contain it. It sounds strange in this room, in this life, in this version of me that has been composure and calculation for four years. It sounds like something I forgot I owned.

Marcello looks at me when I laugh. Just looks, the way he looked at me arriving in Sicily—like he's registering a thing he intends to remember. The expression lasts three seconds, then he stands, rolls his sleeves down one precise turn.

"Donatello has the Warsaw confirmation," he says. "Come."

The confirmation is a photograph taken at a distance. A window on the second floor of a Warsaw building. In it, blurred but unmistakable to me—the particular tilt of a head, the line of a jaw, the light hair that matches mine —is Katya.

I press my fingers to the photograph and cannot speak for a moment.

Alive. Twenty-one months after the van took her from our yard in the snow, my sister Katya is alive in a second-floor room in Warsaw. I'm looking at proof of it in a Sicilian villa with a Lucchese capo standing three feet behind me.

Faustino is at the operations table laptops, maps, files arranged with the precision of a man whose mind categorizes constantly. He meets my eyes when I look up, and he gives me a single nod. Donatello stands by the window, arms folded, and he gives me nothing. But his jaw sets in the way I have learned means something has engaged the part of him that solves problems with his hands.

Marcello comes to stand beside me. Not behind, not opposite, but beside. His shoulder almost touching mine, looking at the same photograph, and his voice when he speaks is low and even and as certain as the stone walls of this villa.

"We bring her here. Both operations—Warsaw and the farm—run at the same time, so there's no warning sent ahead." His eyes stay on the photograph. "I need your help on the farm, Gala. Your father won't open the door for my men. He will for you."

I have been waiting for this—I knew it was coming. I'm the best intelligence asset for this operation, and I knew from the moment Faustino spread the maps that they would need me to be more than a woman in a guest room.

"Yes," I say. Before he can qualify it, before he can soften the ask with reassurances I don't need. "Yes. I go. I open the door."

He turns to look at me. Searching, the way he searched my face in the garden—looking for the fear underneath the yes, checking that the agreement is real and not performed.

Marcello finds the fear. He sees it. He also sees what is underneath it.

"Good," he says simply.

Paolina appears in the doorway with Cosima on her hip and reads the room in one sweep—the photograph, my face, the set of the men's shoulders—and says nothing. She comes to stand beside me, and her free hand finds mine and squeezes once. Cosima holds out the rabbit.

With both hands, I take it, and for a moment, I think I have a plan. I have people beside me. I have a photograph of my sister alive in a window in Warsaw.

And I have something I have not had since I was eight years old, standing in the farmhouse kitchen watching my mother hang gold stars on the wall.

I have something that might be hope.

I hand the rabbit back to Cosima with the gravity it deserves. She nods. The operation begins.

CHAPTER 8

 *arcello*

THE GYM IS UNDERGROUND—ONE level below the villa's main floor, carved into the hillside itself, the stone walls keeping it cool even in the heat. I've been down here since midnight. The heavy bag hangs from its chain. I've been introducing it to my fists for the better part of two hours with a focus that has nothing to do with training and everything to do with the fact that if I stay still my mind goes to her.

I work combinations. Left hook, right cross, body shot, repeat. The chain rattles. My knuckles split on the fourth set. I don't wrap them, and I don't stop. The sting is useful—it gives the energy somewhere to go.

She laughed today.

One genuine laugh, in the library, brief and surprised and entirely unguarded, and it hit me like a fist to the sternum. I've been managing the wanting since London—the tight professional lid I keep on it, the cold logic of wait and she's not ready and this is not the time. The laugh blew the lid clean off, and I've been down here beating myself back to equilibrium ever since.

I want her.

That's simple.

What's not simple is the specific quality of the wanting. It doesn't feel like the appetites I'm accustomed to managing. The clean physical need that women have always been willing to meet and that I have always been able to walk away from.

This wants the laugh as much as the body. Wants the filing gaze and the lifted chin and the way she traces words with her finger and the sound of her Russian accent thickening when she's about to tell the truth. Wants the whole architecture of her, which is dangerous, which is precisely why I'm down here at midnight hitting something instead of going to her room.

Gala is healing. She needs time. She has been through things that require time, and you do not take from a woman who has had too much taken already.

This I know. I also know she's been awake for the last hour. Her footsteps in the hall are recognizable. I know the particular quality of the light under her door. I know she's been standing outside the gym door for approximately four minutes.

I stop. Let my hands fall. The bag swings on its chain and goes still.

The door opens.

She stands in an oversized T-shirt that belongs to Gemma and a pair of shorts, hair loose down her back, bare feet on the stone floor. The gym light is the low amber of the wall sconces, and it turns the ash blonde of her hair to something warmer and catches the dove gray of her eyes when they find mine across the room.

She isn't pretending she wandered down here by accident. That chin is level. That gaze is direct.

I'm shirtless and bleeding slightly at the knuckles. My chest is heaving. I have approximately no composure left, which is inconvenient.

"You couldn't sleep," she says. Not a question.

"No."

Her eyes move down to my hands—the split knuckles, the blood. Something crosses her face. Not alarm. Something more complicated than alarm.

"What were you thinking about?" she asks.

You. Every version of you I've catalogued since London. Your laugh. The way you ate that first meal like someone rationing. Your hands on the wall of the garden. The sound you made when I told you Katya was alive.

Aloud, I say, "Nothing useful."

She holds my gaze for a long moment. Then she crosses the room.

She stops in front of me—close enough that I can smell her. The warm, clean scent that's purely her underneath everything else. She lifts one hand and places it flat against my chest.

Over my heart. Her palm is cool against the heat of my skin. She can feel it hammering.

Gala.

I cover her hand with mine—not to move it, simply to tell her I feel it too. I keep my eyes on hers.

"Tell me to stop," I say. "And I stop."

She looks at me for one more second. Then she steps closer, closes the remaining distance, and presses her mouth to mine.

*G*ALA

HE TASTES of effort and something dark and clean. The first touch of his mouth is so careful—so deliberately, precisely careful, the way he does everything—that something in me clenched since London simply opens.

Oh.

I kissed Marcello Lucchese first. I want to be clear about that, even inside my head—this was not taken from me. I gave it. I chose it.

I stood in the doorway for four minutes, considering reasons to go back to bed. Every one of them was sound, and none of them was strong enough. Because the sound of the chain rattling and the knowledge that he was down here at midnight hitting something, and the look on his face when I made him laugh today added up to one conclusion that no amount of survival math could argue against.

I want him.

His hands come up to my face—both of them, slow, cradling my jaw with a gentleness somehow more devastating than force would be. He angles my head and deepens the kiss and makes a sound low in his throat that I feel everywhere. The part of my brain that has been running threat assessments since the van goes quiet for the first time in months.

Quiet. Just—quiet. No calculations. No exits. Just this.

He breaks the kiss and looks at me. The careful neutrality is gone, the professional composure stripped off, and what's underneath is something vast and direct and aimed entirely at me.

"I'm going to take my time," he says. His voice has dropped to something low and rough that moves through me like a current. "Tell me if you want me to stop."

He will ask. Every time. I already know this about him— the asking isn't performance, it's architecture. It's how he's built.

"Don't stop," I say.

Marcello

· · ·

I take my time.

The T-shirt goes first—I lift it over her head and she lets me, arms raised, and then she's standing in the amber gym light in just the shorts. I take her in the way I take in any situation that demands full attention, completely, without rushing to the next thing.

She's extraordinarily beautiful in a way that has nothing to do with the stage they put her on—this is not performance, this is a woman in low light on a Sicilian hillside who has stopped being afraid of what she wants.

Mine. Not because I took her. Because she is standing here.

I bring her against me slowly, one hand at the small of her back, the other coming up to her hair—and she makes a soft sound when our skin meets, a sound of surprised pleasure, like she wasn't expecting warmth. My hand tightens in her hair, gently tilting her head back, and her throat is pale in the amber light. I put my mouth there, and she exhales—long, slow, like something she's been holding for a very long time.

I take her mouth again, deeper, one hand in her hair and the other traveling the length of her—the curve of her waist, the flare of her hip, the soft warmth of her skin.

She arches into my hand, her own hands gripping my arms, nails pressing in. Not to push me away. The opposite.

"Marcello—" she starts.

"I have you," I tell her. Against her mouth. "I have you."

I walk her back to the training mat and lower her down. I plank over her and eyes roam her face. Eyes look back at mine, no wariness in them right now, no calculation, no armor. Just her. Just this.

This is what she looks like when she isn't surviving. This is what she looks like when she's simply living.

I drop my head and put my mouth to the curve of her neck, her collarbone, the swell of her breast, and she gasps and arches as her fingers thread into my hair. I take my time. Every inch of her is a thing I intend to learn properly, and I have all night. She deserves to be worshipped by someone who understands the difference between taking and being given.

When my mouth reaches her stomach, she makes a sound that tightens everything in me. I trace lower, and her hips rise as her hands grip the mat.

"Look at me," I command.

Those gray eyes find mine.

I hold them. And I take care of her.

GALA

I HAVE NEVER FELT this way. Not with a man who asks with his hands before he asks with words, not with a man who watches your face like it contains all the information he needs and adjusts accordingly. Our farm gave me nothing of this. The van gave me terror of it. The auction stage gave me the threat of it.

This is none of those things.

His mouth on me is deliberate and certain and unhurried.

I come apart completely—the first time with a sound I barely recognize as mine, high and unguarded, my hands in his hair—and he does not stop, works me through it, watches my face with those dark intent eyes until I stop shaking. Then he rises above me again, both hands framing my face. His weight is warm and solid, real. I reach for him.

"Tell me," he murmurs against my mouth.

"Yes," I say. "Now. Please."

He shifts, positioning himself.

I feel the cool, unexpected touch of metal—a piercing —and my breath catches.

His eyes sharpen immediately, watching my face.

"That—" I start.

"I know," he says, low and rough. "Tell me if it's too much."

It is not too much. The absolute opposite of too much.

"Oh. Oh, that is—"

He moves slowly, reading every breath I take, and when he is fully inside me, we both go still. The amber light and the stone walls and his forehead against mine.

Both of us breathing, adjusting to the weight of the moment.

Full. Claimed. But the claiming goes both ways—I can feel it. He is not taking. We are taking each other.

"Gala," he says. My name in his mouth, in the dark, in Italian-accented English with the weight of a man who does not say things carelessly.

"Move," I tell him.

Marcello

She undoes every piece of discipline I own.

Every response honest, every sound real, her hands on me like she's been waiting for somewhere to put all the strength she's been holding in check. She comes apart a second time when I reach between us and find the angle that makes her gasp my name and grip the mat, and I follow her over the edge with a groan I don't bother containing because there's no one in this room to perform for. It's just us. Just the amber light and the stone walls and this woman and me.

Afterward, we stay as we are, her head on my chest, my hand moving slowly through the fall of her hair. The gym is quiet. Somewhere above us the villa sleeps.

Her breathing slows. Her hand lies flat against my ribs, feeling my heartbeat come down.

Then she speaks.

"Even though you took me against my will, thank you for helping me. You're not a monster like the men I've known."

I'm still.

She's giving her trust to me now—here, after this, in this room. The timing is not accidental. She's decided I am the right person.

"You're welcome."

She looks at me for a long moment. Something moves in her eyes—the last calculation, the final piece of the assessment she has been running on me since London, arriving at its answer. Whatever she finds satisfies some-thing, because the eyes soften. Not the softening of defeat. The softening of decision.

She's decided. I can feel it. Whatever the decision is—she's made it.

She lays her head back on my chest without speaking. Her hand presses flat against my heart.

We stay there in the amber light until the stone walls pale toward dawn. I do not sleep, and I do not want to, because I would rather be awake in this than asleep in anything else.

Ti amo.

I do not say it yet. Not because it isn't true—because she is not ready to receive it. But I know it now, here in this gym on this hillside, with this woman's hand over my heart in the dark.

I will dismantle a pig farm in Russia and a Bratva network across three countries and tear a hole in the world if I have to. And when it's done, I will say it out loud.

And she will say it back. I am as certain of this as I have ever been of anything.

The dawn comes in. I hold her tighter.

ala

THE OPERATIONS ROOM smells of espresso and the particular charged air of men who are very good at dangerous things and are in the process of planning one. Maps cover the long table—satellite images of the Perm Krai region printed on heavy paper, Warsaw street grids with handwritten annotations in Faustino's precise script, photographs of the farm that I have not looked at directly yet because I am not ready and I know it and I file that knowledge and keep my eyes on the men instead.

Marcello is at the head of the table. He has a quality in rooms like this that he doesn't quite have anywhere else

—a completeness, like a weapon taken off a shelf and is now being used for its actual purpose.

The baby face sharpens. The mink brown eyes go still differently, not the watchful stillness of a man in a garden at dusk but the operational stillness of a man for whom this room is his most natural environment.

He uses his hands when he talks, quick illustrative gestures as he speaks rapid Italian to Faustino and Donatello, and watching him I understand for the first time what the baby face actually is—misdirection. The face that makes rooms underestimate him while the hands and the mind and the absolute unhurried certainty of him are already three moves ahead.

Last night was not a mistake. Whatever it complicates, it was not a mistake.

He held me until the stone walls went pale. He didn't make it smaller than it was. Nor did he make it about himself. He simply stayed, and in staying said everything he has not yet said out loud.

Faustino sees me in the doorway and tips his head toward the chair at Marcello's right. Not the chair at the far end, but the observer's position. The chair at his right hand—the seat that means you're part of this, not an object of it. I cross the room and sit in it and Donatello, who's leaning over the Warsaw street grid with a red pen, glances at me with those dark Romano eyes and gives me a look that contains approximately eight separate observations about the current state of affairs, none of which he voices because Donatello Romano is constitutionally incapable of saying anything that doesn't need to be said.

Marcello glances at me. One look, brief—his eyes doing what they always do, encompassing, accounting, checking whether I'm all right without asking out loud because asking out loud would make it a thing and making it a thing would compromise the operational efficiency of the next two hours. Something in them warms by one degree, and then he returns to the map.

"Good morning," he says, in Italian, deliberately, without looking up from the satellite image of the Perm Krai region.

"Buongiorno," I say back. My accent is better than it was two weeks ago. His mouth moves at the corner.

Faustino clears his throat. The briefing begins.

Two operations. Simultaneous. That's the structure of it. As Faustino lays it out, I follow every piece with the attention of someone who's been planning a version of this since she was fourteen years old standing outside a bedroom door in the dark.

Warsaw: retrieval of Katya from the Bratva-adjacent safe house on the Praga side of the river. Donatello leads a four-man team. Entry at 2 a.m. local time, when the building will be at minimum occupancy and the guards most likely to be at their least alert. The goal is extraction with minimum engagement—though engagement is anticipated, and Donatello's equipped his team for it the way he always equipped it, comprehensively.

Faustino traces the Warsaw street grid with one

finger, showing the approach routes. The safe house is on a block with two exits—one to the main road, one to a service alley that connects to a parallel street where they'll stage the extraction vehicles. Simple in concept, meaning the variables are all in the execution, which means this is exactly the operation Donatello was built for.

Russia: simultaneous extraction of Irina, Syuzanna, Tasha, Borya, and Yeva from the farm. Faustino leads that team himself—six men, vehicles standing by at a staging point eight kilometers from the property. The farm is remote enough that the nearest neighbors are unlikely to be involved. The window is the same 2 a.m. slot, which, accounting for time zones, runs parallel to the Warsaw operation within a margin of four minutes. Four minutes is acceptable. Four minutes is nothing.

Then Faustino says, "The problem."

He says it without emphasis, the way Faustino says everything—flat, factual, the information presented without theatrical framing. The problem is that the farm has one approach road, one lane wide, visible from the farmhouse kitchen window for three hundred meters.

A man named Borislav Zhukova who has spent four years in that farmhouse developing the particular hyper-vigilance of a man who has done things that require watching for consequences. Unknown vehicles in the night, on that road, approaching that house—he will barricade. He will drag the people inside to the most defensible position before Faustino's team can reach them, and the most defensible position is the interior rooms, and interior rooms complicate extraction.

Faustino does not say he will harm them. He does not say it because saying it aloud in this room, with me sitting in the chair at Marcello's right hand, is unnecessary. Everyone in this room knows what Borislav Zhukova has been doing to the people in that farmhouse. The report was twelve pages long. They've all read it.

The room is quiet for three seconds.

"I'm ready to go," I say.

My voice comes out steady. I've been preparing this sentence since they confirmed Warsaw. Since the moment I saw Katya's blurred silhouette in the second-floor window and understood that the plan was real and moving and that my role in it was not optional, regardless of what anyone in this room preferred.

Marcello nods.

"You stay on comms at all times," he says. "You have a signal—three clicks—and if you give it, my men come through that door before he can breathe. Do not go inside. Do not go anywhere on that property without my men in position first. You say what you need to say at the door, you step back, and you let the team work."

I nod.

He looks at me for another moment. Something in his face is doing what it does when he's containing something he would prefer to act on but has decided—correctly, rationally—not to act on. The something is unmistakable now that I know what his face looks like without the management. Worry. Specific, personal, directed at me.

He's worried about me walking back to a pig farm in Russia. Marcello Lucchese, who has never in his adult life displayed fear for himself, who walked into a Mayfair auction room and lifted me off a stage with the calm certainty of a man rearranging furniture, is worried about me.

I file this. Hold it carefully. I don't let it show on my face because showing it will make this harder for both of us, and we have work to do.

"Good," he says and turns back to the map.

Good. One word. What it contains acceptance, reluctance, respect, and the particular quality of a man who has decided protecting someone sometimes means trusting them to protect themselves.

I know, I think. I know what that cost you. Thank you.

THE BRIEFING CONTINUES for another hour. Routes, timing, communication protocols, extraction vehicle positions, medical assets staged at the Catania airport for Katya's arrival. Faustino has thought of everything, which is his function and his nature. The man whose name means lucky is the least lucky person in any room because he plans for every contingency so luck doesn't have to show up.

I contribute what I know: the farm's layout from memory, the positions of the outbuildings, the fact

Borislav sleeps in the back bedroom and will take at minimum forty-five seconds to reach the front door from a standing start.

Faustino makes notes.

Donatello marks the approach positions on the satellite image.

Marcello listens to everything I say without interrupting. When I'm done, he looks at Faustino.

"She knows this property better than the satellite," he says. "Adjust the positions accordingly."

Faustino nods and adjusts.

He deferred to my intelligence. In his own operations room, in front of his men, he adjusted the plan based on what I know. He did not check with Donatello or look for confirmation. He simply accepted it.

I've been in this room for ninety minutes, and I feel more like myself than I have since the van.

Paolina finds me in the garden afterward. She appears around the corner of the east wing with Cosima and reads my demeanor—my face, the set of my shoulders, the particular quality of the afternoon light on a woman who has just agreed to walk back into a place she escaped —and she sits beside me on the stone wall and says nothing for a full minute.

The minute is a gift. I use it.

Then she says, "I need to tell you something about the night Donatello brought me to his private island. About what it cost me to decide to trust him, and what I found when I did."

She talks for a while, there in the lemon-tree light—about what it is to be taken by a man you had no reason to trust, and what it costs to decide to trust him anyway, and the specific terror of finding that the decision was correct. About the night she discovered she was pregnant, and the night Cosima was born, and the morning she woke up on the private island and understood that the life she was building there was actually, genuinely hers. Not a comfortable cage. Hers.

She talks the way she talks about everything—with the frankness of a woman who has survived something and sees no reason to make it prettier than it was. I listen the way I have learned to listen in this villa—completely, without planning my response.

Then she says, "Whatever you need to do on that farm, I understand. I won't ask what it is. But I understand."

She does not ask. She already knows.

She knows because she looked at Donatello the same way I look at Marcello—with the particular mixture of clarity and terrified hope of a woman who has found something real in an impossible place and is still not entirely sure she may keep it.

I may keep it. I decided this in the gym at midnight and deciding it again here, in the lemon-tree light, with Paolina beside me.

That evening at dinner I watch the table the way I always watch it now—not for threats, not for exits, but for the texture of it, the warmth, the way this collection of people has arranged itself into something that functions like a family even though it assembled itself from loyalty and history and the particular stubbornness of people who refused to let the worst things be the final things.

Gemma tells a story about something that happened in Catania that afternoon that involves a fish market and a misunderstanding about directions and escalates rapidly into something involving a Vespa that I do not follow entirely because my Italian is still catching up but that makes Donatello laugh—a real laugh, deep and short and slightly surprised, the laugh of a man who does not laugh often and forgets to manage the sound when he does.

Paolina catches my eye across the table. She raises her wine glass a fraction of an inch.

Marcello refills mine. He does it without looking at me, mid-conversation with Faustino about something operational, his hand finding my glass and filling it by instinct the way I imagine he has filled the same glass in the same way every night for years, except that my glass has only been at this table for three weeks and he has already learned where it sits.

I love him.

I will not tell him yet. Not until the farm is done and my sisters are safe and Borislav Zhukova is dead in his own barn. Because if Marcello knows I love him before this operation, he'll fold the knowledge into his risk calculations in a way that will cost him something I don't want to cost him—the clarity he needs to run this cleanly. He'll think about me instead of the mission, and the mission requires his full attention.

After. Everything honest, after.

He glances at me. His eyes find mine for one second —a check, a confirmation, the private language we've been building since London. I hold his gaze for the count of it and give him what I've learned he reads in my face as *I am all right, here, with you.*

He looks back at Faustino. The conversation continues.

I eat everything on my plate. Every last bite. No rationing. No saving for later. All of it, here, now, at this table, with these people, in this life that I chose and will keep choosing every morning I wake up in it.

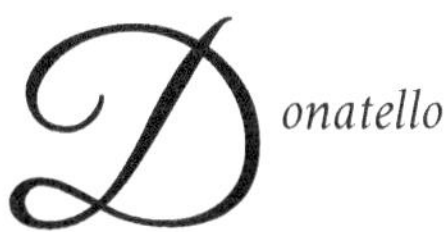onatello

WARSAW at 2 a.m. is the color of old pewter—the streets between the Soviet-era blocks slicked with rain that fell an hour ago and hasn't dried, the orange sodium lights making halos in the wet air, the city's nighttime sounds reduced to the distant thrum of a tram two streets over and the particular urban silence that fills in between. I've operated in eighteen cities across four continents. Warsaw at night has a specific quality to it, a weight to the dark that older cities carry—the weight of things that happened here and not forgotten.

I'm in position in the alley across from the safe house.

Four-story building, pre-war construction, the kind of thick-walled block that absorbs sound efficiently and designed with that specific utility in mind. Two guards visible on the ground floor through the smoked glass of the entrance—not Bratva soldiers, hired muscle. The security arrangement that suggests the Bratva want this location to be low-profile enough that their own men aren't standing outside it. Two more on the second floor, confirmed by my contact who did the walk-by at midnight. Minimal movement on the upper levels for the last ninety minutes.

He confirms what the building registration already suggested—the safe house is Sobol's operation, running under one of his Cyprus shell companies. The same network that ran the Mayfair auction. The same man whose name Faustino put on Marcello's desk in London. We're dismantling Yuri Sobol's European circuit one location at a time, and he doesn't yet know how much of it the Luccheses already own.

Good. Let him find out slowly. Slow discovery is more expensive than fast discovery.

A soldier is at my left, close enough that I can hear him breathe—slow and measured, the operational breathing of a man who's been doing this since he was fifteen and his body has long since stopped treating danger as an exception. His skullcap blocks the rain. His eyes focus on the second-floor window—the one where the contact confirmed the Bratva placed Katya. The one that has shown a faint backlight for the last twenty minutes, which means someone is awake up there.

Marcello, Faustino, and Gala are on a flight to the

Perm Krai region right now with six men, landing in Perm in forty minutes and driving two hours to the farm staging point. I know this because Faustino sent a two-word message ninety minutes ago, on schedule. That's all I will hear from him until the operation is complete. Faustino does not narrate his work.

Two operations. One clock. Four minutes of acceptable variance between them.

I reach into my left breast pocket without looking down. My fingers find what they're looking for and press it flat for two seconds, then release. Cosima's photograph. I've done this before every operation since the night she was born—Catania and Palermo and London and twice in New York, always the same: two seconds, flat palm, release.

Two minutes, the soldier says. Low, Italian, barely a breath.

I check my Glocks. Both chambers full. Both safeties disengaged. The weight of them is as familiar as my own hands. I've been carrying these specific weapons since I was nineteen years old, and I know their balance the way I know my heartbeat, which is currently steady at approximately fifty-five beats per minute, which is where it goes before an operation. Not slow—precise. My body has learned the difference between rest and readiness.

One minute.

The clock strikes 2 a.m.

We move.

THE GROUND FLOOR goes fast and clean. Both guards down in under twenty seconds, subdued rather than eliminated because low-profile matters, zip-tied and gagged in the service corridor before they process what's in the room with them. My men know how to do this.

First floor cleared. Second floor stairwell.

The hallway on the second floor is narrow and low-lit, with the fluorescent overhead flickering at one end. Three doors. The contact said the third. We move to it.

The soldier tries the handle. Locked. He looks at me. I nod.

The door comes off the frame in one movement—his shoulder, his weight, the particular application of force that sixteen years of MMA training makes look effortless. It is not effortless. It is the product of ten thousand hours of work compressed into a single instant.

The room is small and smells of confinement—damp, stale air, the specific human smell of people kept in a place too long with insufficient ventilation. Three women on cots along the far wall. Thin blankets. A single window, painted shut. A plastic chair. No other furniture.

This is where they kept her. For how long before Warsaw? How many rooms like this, in how many cities, since the van took her from a yard in Russia fourteen months ago.

We will dismantle every node of this network. This is not strategic. This is personal.

One woman is standing at the window. Back to us, hands pressed to the glass, the particular posture of someone who has been standing at windows for a long time, hoping for something different on the other side.

Ash blonde hair. Nearly waist-length. The particular tilt of the head—I recognize this head.

Katya.

She turns at the sound of the door coming off its frame. Her face moves through three complete expressions in under two seconds. First, the raw animal terror of someone who has learned that loud sounds in this room mean something bad—the flinch, the body coiling back, every survival instinct firing at once. Then a freezing stillness, processing, reading the room—the men, the tactical gear, no one is moving toward her with intent. Then the third thing, the one that undoes me slightly, a collapsing, a questioning. The face of someone who has stopped allowing themselves to hope because hope costs too much and is now being asked, against every learned instinct, to hope anyway

"Romano," I say. "Tell her."

My soldier steps forward and speaks in Russian, low and even, "Your sister Gala sent us. You're going home."

Katya's legs collapse.

I'm across the room before she reaches the floor—reflexes catching her at the shoulders and holding her up with the same steadiness I apply to everything. Nothing spoken, explained, or reassured. I hold her upright and let her feel she's held and wait.

She grips my forearm with both hands. Her knuckles go white.

There it is. That is the grip of a woman who has been falling for fourteen months and has just found something solid.

The other two women in the room sit up on their cots now, watching us with the wary calculation of people who have learned not to move too fast when things change. I look at them. I look at the soldier.

He gives me a single nod.

"All three," I say. "We leave no one in this hellhole."

We're in the vehicles and moving inside eleven minutes of entry. Eleven minutes from breaching the door to three women in SUVs headed for the airport, which is eighteen seconds slower than our operational target and acceptable given that two of the three women required physical support on the stairs.

The hired muscle in the service corridor was still zip-tied and conscious when we left, which means the Bratva will know about this within three hours. Three hours are sufficient. We'll be in Sicilian airspace before they assemble a response.

Katya is in the car with me and the team medic.

He gave her a light sedative—not enough to disorient, enough to take the edge off the shaking that has not stopped since the room.

Four times she's asked for Gala. The Russian coming out in fragments around the sedative's fog, and each time I've told the medic to tell her she's safe, she sent us, you'll see her by morning.

The medic tells her. She subsides each time. Then, after a few minutes, asks again.

I would answer that question a hundred times. I would fly to Warsaw a hundred times for the particular sound of a sister asking for her sister.

My phone goes off at 2:17 a.m. Warsaw time. Faustino.

The call lasts forty seconds. When it ends, I sit with the phone in my hand for a moment and look out at the Warsaw streets going past the window. The old city, visible now as we move toward the airport, its rebuilt spires and its careful facades, the particular stubborn beauty of a place that was razed and rebuilt itself and went on.

Done. Both operations. Every name on the list. The farm secured, the family out, and Borislav Zhukova zip-tied to a post in a barn, waiting.

Waiting for Gala.

CHAPTER 11

ala

THE DIRT TRACK hasn't changed. That's what strikes me first. The track leads from the approach road to the farmhouse, rutted and pale in the moonlight, edged with the same scrub pine and the same patches of frozen mud for as long as I can remember.

Everything else has changed. The black SUVs moving slowly along it, Marcello's men in tactical gear, the armed presence that has remade this landscape into something his. Yet the track itself is exactly as it was the morning the van drove me away. I looked back through the rear window, and I memorized it because I knew I was going to need it.

I look at it now through the windshield, and I feel nothing surprises me. No sentimentality, no grief for the girl who walked this track to the village and dreamed of leaving. Only a clean, settled certainty that I've been building toward this moment since I was fourteen years old, and it has arrived, and I am ready.

Marcello's hand rests on the seat between us. Not on my hand. Available.

I don't take it. Not yet. I need my hands for what comes next.

The convoy stops fifty meters from the farmhouse. Faustino's men are already in position. I can see them from the SUV. The sightlines established, the perimeter locked. Two men at the corners of the building. Two more at the back exit. Everything arranged so nothing leaves through any door except the front one.

Except me. I leave through the front door. That is my role in this. I claimed it two days ago in the villa in Sicily when Marcello laid the plan on the table and I said, I go to the door. He looked at me for a long moment. Then he nodded once and did not argue, because he understands what this is and what it requires.

"Are you ready?"

His voice is firm. But his eyes concern fills his eyes.

This time, I clasp his hand and squeeze it.

"Yes, I can do this," I say. "I need to do this, Marcello."

"Bene." He returns my squeeze. Fury replaces the worry. "I'm right here."

"Thank you."

I step out of the SUV. Determination straightens my spine.

The cold hits first. The specific cold of the Perm Krai in the early morning, the kind that has teeth and doesn't apologize for them. My breath fogs. My feet find the ground, and I walk toward the farmhouse without looking back, because looking back is not part of this.

The farmhouse is smaller than I remember it. This is the thing no one tells you about returning to the places that made you. They shrink. The scale recalibrates against the person you have become. What was enormous is simply a building in a field, weathered boards and a sagging roof with thin smoke from the chimney. He's awake beside the lit stove. Some habits are the same in monsters as in ordinary men.

I stop at the door.

"Papa!"

My stomach churns using. A term reserved for a man of honor. Borislav Zhukova is no man of honor. He's a monster. A monster I will kill tonight.

I knock. Three times. The knock of a person who fears nothing.

A pause. The sound of movement inside—heavy footsteps, the creak of old floorboards I know the exact location of. The door opens.

He fills the doorframe. He's heavier than I remember, the red face puffier, the ice-chip eyes slower to focus. He looks at me, and his face goes through three stages in one second: confusion, recognition, and then—underneath both of them—fear. A thin, desperate thread of it, there before he can bury it under the bluster.

He's afraid the men brought me back. His eyes scan the darkness. Seeing no one, that ugly sneer lifts the corner of his mouth. Eyes narrow, glittering with that rage.

He opens his mouth.

Before the first word is out, Faustino steps from the corner of the building and takes him by the arm—not roughly, not with theatrics, with the complete professional certainty of a man who has done this a thousand times and requires no help.

Borislav twists and shouts, the Russian nasty and familiar. The same words he used when we failed to meet his standards, the same register of authority he deployed my entire life over people who had no choice but to absorb it.

He has a choice now. He can walk to the barn with Faustino, or he will drag him.

Faustino says something quietly. Borislav stops struggling. They walk toward the barn.

I watch them go. Then I turn back to the house.

I call their names one at a time, the way I called them when we were children and it was safe to come out. Irina. Syuzanna. Tasha.

A beat of silence.

Irina comes first. She is thinner than I remembered. The months since I left carved into her face in ways that photographs from Faustino's surveillance had not prepared me for. She wears her gray coat, and she looks at me, and her mouth opens, but nothing comes out because there are no words sufficient for this unexpected reunion.

I cross the distance between us and take her into my arms.

She holds on hard. Her whole body shakes the way bodies shake when they have been holding something for too long and finally allowed to set it down. I hold her back with everything I have. I say her name against her hair.

"It's over, Irina. I have you. I promise."

Syuzanna comes next, wrapping her arms around us both, and then the children—Borya and Yeva, wide-eyed and overwhelmed, tucked against their mother's legs until Irina reaches down and pulls them in.

Tasha comes last. She doesn't rush, doesn't run. Instead, she walks toward me with the deliberate certainty of a child who's decided and will not be reconsidered. She wraps both arms around my waist and presses her face against my shoulder, and holds on.

No sound. But she is here. She is holding on. She came when I called, and this is everything.

Behind me I hear Marcello moving, the quiet direction of men who understand their role in this moment—be invisible, give us the yard, manage the perimeter without pressing their presence into what is happening between these women in front of a farmhouse in the Perm Krai. SUV doors open. Marcello speaks to his men in low Italian. The machinery of extraction operates around us, requiring nothing from us.

When I lift my face from my sister's hair, I find Marcello watching with those mink brown eyes that miss nothing and, since London, aimed at me with the specific attention of a man paying the regard that cannot be faked. He is not managing me. He's witnessing me. There is a difference I've been learning for weeks.

He moves toward the SUVs. His men guide my sisters —gently, without force, Irina with the children, Syuzanna, Tasha last, each of them handed in with the care of people instructed to treat them accordingly and follow that instruction to the letter because all follow Marcello Lucchese's instructions to the letter.

I watch my family get into the vehicles. Safe. Warm. Out.

Then I turn to Marcello.

"The barn," I say.

He looks at me for a moment. Then he nods and walks beside me.

The barn smells the same. That is the first thing. The particular smell of damp straw and cold wood and livestock that gets into old buildings and never fully leaves.

I know every board of this place. I've fed pigs here and hidden here when the sounds from the bedroom were too much to remain inside the house for. I know the exact creak of the hinges, which I hear now as Marcello pushes the door open and steps in ahead of me, his hand going to his hip as he does—not drawing the weapon, checking it, the automatic assessment of a trained man entering an enclosed space.

Borislav is at the post in the center. Faustino zip-tied his wrists behind it. The same post where we tethered pigs, where Katya and I used to do our lessons in the summer when it was cooler than the house. His ice-chip eyes find me in the doorway, and his face tries again for authority, the expression he has deployed my entire life, the one that was supposed to make me smaller.

It does not land.

He speaks.

"Gryaznaya shlyukha!"

I ignore his attempt to shame me by calling me a dirty whore.

"Sporco bastardo—"

I raise my hand to stop Marcello. He spits more curses, but respects my request.

Borislav's eyes shift to him, assessing, calculating. His lip curls. His tirade continues.

He shouts everything wrong with me, everything wrong with my mother, the daughters she gave him instead of sons.

I know every word. I let him say it all because each word seals his fate further. They increase my power now in a way it never was when I was fourteen and small enough for him to simply override. I am not small enough anymore.

When he runs out of curses, I speak.

I tell him what he is. Not as an accusation, but as a

record. Stated into the cold barn air, the specific accounting of a man who sold his daughters to settle his debts and called it discipline, who broke a family that trusted him and called it strength, who created the silence in Tasha and called it her flaw. I say it all. Clearly, without performance. Not for him. He is not the audience. For my mother. For Irina. For Katya in Warsaw. For Tasha. For the girl I was, lying awake counting the days.

He tries to speak again.

Marcello steps forward and places the gun in my hand. Handle first. His eyes meet mine over it, and in them I see the thing that has been there since the auction stage. The fury on my behalf, contained, steady. The fury of a man who will burn things down and has been waiting for me to decide what gets burned.

Marcello steps back. He does not leave. He remains inside, witnessing this the way it should be.

"Net... podozhdi! Chto ty delayesh'? Net..."

His sputtering for me to stop adds fuel to the fire burning within me.

I raise the gun.

My father continues to beg.

I ignore his pleas and aim the gun at his crotch.

"Net—"

He screams as the bullet tears through the penis and balls that hurt my mother and Irina.

Satisfaction lifts the corners of my mouth. I step closer.

"Monsters die terrible deaths," I murmur in Russian in his ear as I press the gun to his forehead.

I step back enough to stare into his wide eyes filled with fear and pain I put there.

One shot between them.

Then, once through the heart.

The Lucchese way. Two shots. Certain and complete, because certainty is a kindness even at the end, and a man who understands what it means to do something difficult correctly taught me this.

The barn quiets.

A relief so profound, my legs wobble. I lift my eyes to the heavens and vow never to allow anyone to harm my family again. A hand on my lower back grounds me.

Marcello takes the Glock, smooth and unhurried, and holsters it, and that is all. We walk out without a backward glance.

The cold is the same cold as before, and I breathe it in and it is simply cold. Weather. The world continuing.

The SUV's door opens. Irina looks up from inside, and I climb in beside her. She takes my hand with both of hers, and Syuzanna is on my other side. Borya is asleep against Yeva in the third row with Tasha next to the window, looking out at the farm as the vehicle moves.

I watch my sister watch the farm recede.

The dirt track goes under the wheels. The same rutted track, the same scrub pine, the same frozen mud. I memorized it once through a rear window because I knew I would need it. I do not need it anymore. I let it go.

Then Tasha turns from the window.

She looks at me. Those gray eyes—the same gray as mine, the same gray as our mother's—entirely open. No walls in them, no management, just her. The girl who has not spoken in eight years, who has carried her silence like armor, who walked directly to me in the farmhouse yard and held on.

Her mouth opens.

One word. Small and clear and absolutely certain, in the voice of a girl who has decided the world is safe enough now for this.

"Gala."

My name. The first word she's spoken in eight years is my name.

I clasp her hand as tears well in both our eyes.

The sound she makes is not a word. It's something older than words, the sound of a person who has been holding their breath for a long time finally, completely, exhaling.

The convoy moves along the track and out onto the approach road, leaving the farm behind.

My sisters are with me, and Tasha's voice is in my ear.

It's done. My father dead in the barn. My sisters are in this vehicle. Tasha spoke. Katya safe.

I am finished carrying this.

We are going home.

arcello

THE VILLA HAS NEVER SOUNDED like this.

Three days since Russia and the Lucchese compound in Lucca Sicula contains more noise than it has held since my parents were alive. Children's voices and women's laughter. Gemma running what appears to be a full domestic operation in the kitchen with Irina, who emerged from her first forty-eight hours of sleep and silence with the look of someone cautiously checking whether a thing is real. Paolina has made herself the axis around which the practical elements of this reorganized life rotate: she found Syuzanna a room with a window seat and Tasha a small corner of the library with a beanbag and a basket of notebooks. Cosima has appointed herself Borya's personal guide to the compound and is currently leading him through the kitchen garden with the authority of someone who's been doing this for decades.

Katya is in the medical wing. She's physically present, medically stable, and somewhere inside the specific silence of a person who's been through something that requires over three days to process.

The family doctor says, time. Paolina says, time and presence and no one asking her to be further along than she is. Donatello—who's been to Warsaw and back and has said approximately thirty words about it—simply checks on her twice a day and sets food outside her door and leaves.

I understand this. The language of doing instead of saying. The Romano men are fluent in it.

Luca arrives at noon.

He comes alone—no entourage, no statement, just the black Rolls pulling into the courtyard and my older brother stepping out in a dark suit, eyes that miss nothing moving across the compound in one sweep. Ludovico is behind him—his twin with the identical intense stare that earns them three seconds of silence from everyone they meet, already working as he takes in the yard.

I wait for them in the courtyard. We are not a family that embraces. We are a family that clasps hands and reads each other's faces and says what needs to be said without decoration.

Luca looks at me for a long moment. Then he clasps my hand.

"You started a war," he says. "And won it before I knew it was happening."

I say nothing.

"The Bratva intelligence from Warsaw has given us leverage across three Eastern European territories," he continues. "Flavio has already begun negotiations. They released the cargo holds in Palermo. Tommaso sends his regrets about the auctioneer—apparently the man retired suddenly and is no longer available for comment."

A pause. Something moves in Luca's eyes that's not displeasure.

"Don't do it again without asking me," he says. The same words as before. But the temperature is different.

"Understood," I say. I mean it this time as an agreement between equals rather than a man managing his boss. He hears the difference. His grip tightens once before he releases my hand.

They go inside. Ludo pauses beside me as he passes— that intense stare, the one that women and men both find unsettling in their different ways, fixed on my face.

"The auction girl," he says.

"She stays," I say.

He studies me for three seconds longer than is comfortable. Then a slow nod, the chin dimple shifting with it.

"Tell me about the network," he says. "The Warsaw connection. The routes." He pauses, and something in his tone shifts—still controlled, but with a precision that is too specific, too personal, for standard intelligence gathering. "Everything you have on it."

There's something here he's not saying. Something he knows or is looking for that intersects with the trafficking network in a way that is not purely strategic.

I file it. I'll give him everything we have. And later I'll ask Faustino to monitor what Ludo does with it.

"I'll have Faustino put together a full briefing," I say.

Ludo nods once and goes inside.

I stand in the courtyard for a moment, the afternoon light warm on my face, listening to the compound—the children in the kitchen garden, Gemma's voice rising in Italian from inside, the low rumble of Donatello and Faustino talking near the gate.

Full house. Mine. Every person in there under my roof and my protection, and I feel not the weight of that but the solidity.

This is what it was supposed to feel like. This is what Papa built it for.

I look at the family chapel at the far end of the property. For the first time in five years, I don't look away.

Later, I find her on the terrace at dusk.

She's watching the sea—or the direction of it, the valley and the distant glimmer beyond, the last of the light going off the water. She's wearing one of Gemma's dresses, pale linen, and her hair is loose.

The plumeria pendant I've been carrying in my jacket pocket for two days is very present in my awareness.

She turns when she hears me. Those dove gray eyes

differ from how they were in London—still measuring, still precise. But the wariness has a new quality, lighter, as though the thing it was guarding against has been reclassified.

I sit beside her.

We watch the valley go dark.

"You can leave," I say.

She turns to look at me.

"Take your sisters. I've arranged papers—identities, a house here in Sicily if you want it or wherever you want it, accounts with enough that none of you will ever need anything again."

She stares at me.

"The house in Catania has staff. There are schools. Tasha could see a specialist. Whatever she needs—whatever all of them need—it's arranged."

A long pause. The evening bird starts up in the lemon trees.

"Is that what you want?" she asks.

I turn to look at her fully.

"No," I say. "But it is what you choose."

She's quiet for a moment, looking at my face with the precision that's been cataloguing me since the penthouse. The same measurement, but arrived at now with so much more information. She's read eighteen chapters of me. She knows the handkerchief and the gym and the Warsaw call and the barn door and the fact that I stood inside it, and she knows what all of those things mean.

"I choose to stay," she says.

She leans close. I stay still and let her come.

"Because of your sisters?" I ask. "Because of safety?"

She looks up at me with those eyes that have seen everything and survived it. They're looking at me now without calculation, without armor, without the filing intelligence that has been her primary defense since before I met her.

"Because of you," she says.

GALA

HE KISSES ME.

Both hands at my face the way he always holds me —cupped, deliberate, thumbs at my cheekbones. The kiss is slow and deep and completely unhurried and full of everything that has been building since a Mayfair stage and a locked door and three weeks on a Sicilian hillside and a barn in Russia. All of it is in this kiss. All of what we have been to each other and are becoming.

I chose this. I am choosing this. Not because I am here and he is safe and safety is relative after where I've been. But because this man handed me a gun and stood inside a barn door, and when I killed my father, he held my face and asked for nothing.

I am choosing this because I love him. Because I have been loving him since a library and a handkerchief, and I am done waiting to say it.

He walks me inside, through the terrace door, through the sitting room, to his room—not the guest room where I've been sleeping, his room. And when he closes the door, the world outside becomes very far away.

This differs from the gym. There is no urgency in it, no desperation, no tension that has been building since London finally snapping its leash. This is something with room in it—room to look at each other, room to speak, room for us to know each other entirely and still moving toward each other, anyway.

He undresses me slowly. Not the way you undress something you're taking—the way you unwrap something you've been waiting to see properly. His hands on me are reverent and entirely certain. He watches my face the whole time, and I let him watch, because I have nothing left to hide from him.

When I reach for him, his breath catches. I have found, in the weeks since the gym, that there is a specific pleasure in undoing Marcello Lucchese. The places where composure breaks, the sounds that get through the control, the moments when those mink brown eyes go dark and open. I collect them. I am collecting one now.

Marcello

She undoes me.

Completely and specifically, and with the focused attention of a woman who has been studying me for weeks and knows exactly what she's doing with that information. Her hands on my chest, then lower, and the sound that escapes me is not something I would ordinarily allow, but ordinarily I am not in bed with Gala Zhukova.

I pull her under me and take my time.

Longer this time—no training mat, no urgency, no holding back the words that want to be said. I take her apart piece by piece with my hands and my mouth and the Prince Albert piercing she has strong opinions about. I listen to every sound she makes and give her what each sound asks for. When she comes the first time, she says my name in a tone I'm going to spend the rest of my life trying to earn again.

When I'm inside her, we're both still for a moment—foreheads together, both breathing, the particular holy quality of a moment that is entirely real and entirely chosen.

"Gala," I groan. My voice comes out rough, lower than I intend. I need to say something.

She looks at me. No armor. Just her.

"Ti amo."

The words arrive before I've planned them—pulled

out by the moment, by the particular quality of her eyes in this light, by three weeks of learning her and one barn door and every night I lay awake in this room knowing she was down the hall and the world had arranged itself correctly for the first time since I was twenty-one and a car bomb went off in a Messina street.

She stills beneath me. Her hands press flat against my chest.

Then, quietly, in Russian—words I do not speak but understand because I've spent three weeks learning the sound of her truth:

"*Ya tebya lyublyu.*"

I love you.

I don't need the translation. I knew it in the library when she laughed. Felt it in the garden when she cried. I knew it inside the barn when she turned to the door and her eyes found mine.

I just needed her to know it, too.

I move. She arches. We say everything else without words.

She's asleep against my chest when I produce the pendant. I hold it in the dark and look at it—the gold heart with the family symbol. The plumeria wrapped around the silver dagger, the same pendant Gemma wears, the same one Allegra wears, the tracking device encoded inside it and the three generations of Lucchese women who have worn it before them.

Gala stirs. Her eyes open. She looks at the pendant in my hand and does not speak.

"Every woman in this family wears one," I say. "If you want it."

She sits up slowly. Looks at the pendant, then at my face, then back.

She holds out her hand.

I place it in her palm. She looks at it for a long moment—the gold catching the faint light, the plumeria delicate and exact, the dagger underneath it.

Then she turns and lifts her hair and waits.

I fasten it at her throat. My lips touch the back of her neck and press there for a moment longer than fastening requires.

She covers my hands with hers. Outside, in the compound, everything is still. Below, the valley is dark, and the sea is a darker blue at the horizon. Inside this room the night holds us and asks nothing of us, and we give it nothing back but this.

Mine. Not because I took her. Because she stayed.

I took her from an auction stage, trembling and silent. She was already planning her own salvation, and she needed no one to save her.

Gala didn't need me to save her. She saved herself. She saved her sisters. And she saved the dream of her mother she carried through a pig farm and a van and a London stage and a barn in Russia.

But she let me stand outside the barn door. She let me hold her face when she came out. She let me fasten the pendant at her throat, and she covered my hands with hers.

She let me stay.

CHAPTER 13

ne Month Later
Gala

THE VILLA DIFFERS from a month ago—the heat has
thinned, the lemon trees heavy with fruit that Cosima
has appointed herself the guardian of, permitting
harvesting only on a schedule she alone has determined.
The compound has settled into a shape that makes room
for everyone in it. My family settled in a villa near the
east section—Irina with Borya and Yeva in one wing,
Syuzanna in another room with a window seat and her
first-ever stack of books, Tasha in her library corner
with the notebooks she's begun filling, slowly, with
words.

Words. My sister is writing words.

Katya came out of the medical wing ten days ago. She came out quietly, the way she moves through everything now—testing each floor as though checking whether it will hold. Gemma was there, and Paolina was there, and I was there, and we did not make a ceremony of it, and we did not ask her to be further along than she was.

She sat in the garden that first afternoon and looked at the lemon trees for a long time without speaking, and Cosima came and sat beside her in complete companionable silence, and after a while Katya put her arm around Cosima who did not move and that was that.

She's healing. Not the way she was before. Before is gone. But she's healing into a new shape, and the new shape has room in it for sitting in a Sicilian garden with a child and lemon trees and silence that is not afraid.

I wake early, as I always do now—not from vigilance, but from habit that is slowly becoming preference. The habit of being awake when the light first comes, of having the first hour of the day before anyone else needs anything. I learned this habit on the farm, where the first hour was the only safe one. Here the safety persists past the first hour and into the second, and the third, and the entire day. But I keep the early waking because it has become mine.

Marcello sleeps.

I watch him—the baby face at rest, the hands open, the particular stillness of a man whose waking hours are all motion and attention and forward momentum.

He looks like someone's younger brother. He looks exactly like what he is underneath all of it. The youngest of the four brothers. The one who learned early that he had to hit harder and move faster and be more certain than anyone else in the room. Then he carried that into adulthood and turned it into a weapon. Also, quietly, into the way he holds me when the nightmares come.

They still come. Less often. He has never once made it about him when they do—never asks what they were, never offers solutions. He simply holds on.

I will keep waking early in this house for the rest of my life. I will not always know what to do with the silence and the safety, but I will learn.

We will learn together.

The pendant rests warm against my throat. I touch it in the mornings before I get up, a habit formed in the second week without my noticing—the way you touch something when you are checking it's real. The plumeria and the dagger. Order and love, and the capacity for both at once.

Gemma touched hers the same way the morning I noticed, and caught me watching, and raised her coffee cup without a word.

The kitchen is full by eight. This is the rhythm of the house now—Irina and Gemma have become a collaboration in the kitchen that neither of them planned and both of them take seriously, comparing methods across the language gap with the focused pragmatism of women who understand that feeding people is a form of love.

This morning Irina is laughing at something Gemma has done to a batch of dough. The sound of it is still doing something to my chest—still landing the way it did the first time, like a door opening in a wall.

Tasha appears in the kitchen doorway. She has her notebook under her arm, and her eyes go to me first, the way they always do. I meet them and nod. She crosses the kitchen to the table, sits down, and opens the notebook. She begins to write.

A word. Then another. The pen moves carefully, as though she is relearning the connection between thought and language and is choosing not to rush it.

I bring her tea. She looks up when I set it in front of her, and her mouth moves—not quite a smile yet, but the form of one, the muscles learning the shape.

There you are, Tasha. There you are.

Donatello and Paolina are leaving tomorrow. Their island calls them back—Donatello has operations to run from it, and Paolina has her own life there, the life she's built from a private island and a devoted man and a daughter who names fish. Before she goes, she finds me in the garden.

She doesn't say much. She looks at the pendant, at my face, at the villa behind me with all its noise and life. Then she says, "I'm glad Marcello asked Donatello to call me."

"I am too," I say with a bright smile.

She hugs me properly—moss green eyes warm and raven hair falling forward. She holds on with the sincerity of someone who's decided you're family and means the implications of that word. I hold on back.

When Donatello and Marcello say goodbye, they do it in the courtyard in Italian too fast for me to follow, with the hand-clasp and the weight of thirty years of brotherhood in it. Then Donatello looks at me over Marcello's shoulder and gives me a single nod that contains approximately thirty observations about the state of affairs, all of them approving.

Faustino, who's staying—Faustino is always staying, Faustino is as permanent a feature of this compound as the olive trees—watches the departure from the gate with one raised eyebrow and says nothing.

These men, I think. I'm surrounded by these men, and I am not afraid of a single one of them.

My mother would have liked Faustino. He is exactly the kind of man she would have assigned the most gold stars to.

THE LESSON STARTS at four o'clock.

Tasha's idea. She brought me the notebook three days ago, open to a page where she had written in careful block letters: TEACH ME, underlined twice.

So I teach her.

The way our mother taught me—reading comprehension, then English vocabulary, then mathematics, then history. I use the same progression, the same patience, the same gold stars drawn in the margins when she gets something right. I bought the gold star stickers in Catania.

Tasha looked at the first one for a long time before she put the notebook down and pressed both hands to her face and breathed.

Today we're outside on the low garden wall, the light warm on our shoulders, the notebooks spread between us. Borya and Yeva play in the grass below, narrated by Cosima, who provides a running commentary on everything they do in Italian they don't speak yet and considers this educational.

Tasha works through a reading exercise. Her mouth moves slightly with the words—she's reading silently. But the muscle memory of sound is returning. I can see it. The way the lips shape the syllables even when the voice doesn't come.

The exercise ends. She looks up.

I draw a gold star in the margin. Large. Deliberate.

She looks at the star. Then she looks up at the villa behind us, at the stone walls and the lemon trees and the valley beyond and the distant sea, and her face does the thing it has been slowly, carefully, incrementally doing for a month. It opens.

She reaches up and touches the pendant at my throat. Her fingers trace the plumeria, the dagger.

Then she looks at me. And she says, in a voice that is still finding its shape, rough with disuse but entirely certain, "Home."

I look up, and Marcello is at the garden gate.

He came quietly—I didn't hear him, but Tasha did, I think, because her eyes went to the gate a moment before I looked.

He's standing with one hand on the gatepost, dark suit jacket gone, white shirtsleeves rolled, and he's looking at us the way he looked at me coming off the stairs in Sicily on the first day—registering something he intends to remember.

The lesson. The gold star. Tasha's hand on my pendant. The word she just said.

He heard it. I can see it in his face—the thing that happens when Marcello Lucchese is moved and does not move away from it. Face open. The eyes that miss nothing, full.

He stays at the gate, doesn't come in and interrupt the lesson, and he does not walk away. He stays where he is and watches.

The evening comes down around all of us—the children in the grass, Tasha with her notebook and her new word, the pendant warm at my throat—and he stays.

Tasha writes something in her notebook and holds it up for me to see. One word, the letters careful and deliberate and underlined, GOLD STAR.

I laugh.

It's not an almost-laugh. Not a quiet one. It fills the garden and startles the birds from the lemon trees and Borya and Cosima look up and Yeva, who's been watching the birds with intense concentration, loses her balance and sits down hard in the grass and is immediately fine and outraged about it simultaneously.

From the gate, in Italian, Marcello says something to Faustino that I catch because my Italian has been getting better: something about the birds, and the laugh, and a word I had to look up the first time I heard it—casa. Home.

Home.

Yes.

This is what home sounds like.

THANK you for reading *Taken by the Capo*! If you enjoyed the book, I would so appreciate your review as they make a huge difference for indie authors.

Don't want it to be over? Need more?
Join my newsletter for an exclusive bonus epilogue with
a special addition for this duo!
https://BookHip.com/RZXJHBG

WANT to read more about the Taken Series? Turn the page for a preview of *Taken by the Consigliere: A Dark Mafia Lovers to Enemies to Lovers Romance.*

. . .

BE sure to join my Facebook Group for a community who love my spicy worlds facebook.com/groups/charmainelouisebookscoterie!

For early access to my current works and bonus books, visit my Ream Stories reamstories.com/charmainelouisebooks.

PREVIEW TAKEN BY THE CONSIGLIERIE: A DARK MAFIA LOVERS TO ENEMIES TO LOVERS ROMANCE

Twenty-Three Years Ago
Messina, Sicily

Flavio

I KNOW which bins are good.

The one behind the fish market on the Via Garibaldi is the best one. The restaurant two doors down throws out real food on Tuesday nights—not garbage, actual food, things a person could eat. A lesson I learned four months ago, and I've been coming back every Tuesday since. I know exactly when the kitchen closes. I know how long I have before the rats get there first.

I'm crouching behind the bin with a piece of bread when the boy finds me.

He's clean. That's the first thing I notice. Clean clothes, clean shoes—both of them. We're about the same age. But he looks like he's never had to check a bin in his life, and I can tell just from looking at him he hasn't. He doesn't look scared of me. He doesn't look sorry for me either, the way some grown-ups do when they see me, all soft eyes and then looking away fast like they caught something.

He just looks at me. Like I'm interesting.

"What's your name?" he asks.

"Flavio."

"Where do you live?"

I wave at the harbor. It means everywhere and nowhere. He can figure out the rest.

He looks where I pointed. Then back at me. "Come home with me," he says. "My mother will feed you. She feeds everyone. It's a problem she has."

I think about whether to go. I'm eight years old, and I've learned to think about things like this. What does he want? Will it cost me anything? What happens if it goes wrong?

But he's a kid. He's alone. And the worst thing that happens is someone sends me away at the door, and it wouldn't be the first time.

"All right," I say.

He sticks out his hand like a grown-up. "I'm Luca."

I shake it.

His house is the biggest house I've ever been inside that wasn't a church. It smells like food—real food, garlic and something roasting and bread, all at the same time. The floors are marble and cold under my feet. I only have one shoe. I lost the other one three weeks ago, and

I've been walking around with one shoe ever since because one shoe is still better than no shoes.

A pretty woman with dark hair comes out of the kitchen. She looks at me for a second but doesn't look sorry for me. Instead, she just looks at me like she's deciding something. She says something fast to the person behind her, and then she bends down so her face is at the same level as mine.

"You are welcome here," she says.

Nobody has ever said that to me before. Not like that. Not like they meant it and weren't going to change their mind in five minutes.

A big man comes into the hallway with a face that makes you stand up straight without meaning to. He looks at me the way the woman looked at me—like he's deciding something. Then he puts his hand out.

"Vincenzo," he says.

I shake his hand. He shakes it back as if I'm a person. Not a kid, not a problem, a person. I don't know what to do with that, so I just hold still and try not to show it on my face.

Then I notice the other one.

He's standing in a doorway at the end of the hall, looking exactly like Luca, except he isn't smiling. He's just watching me with these dark eyes, like he's adding something up in his head.

Luca says, "That's Ludovico. My twin. He'll pretend he doesn't like you for about two weeks, then he'll act like he always did. He won't bring up the two weeks."

"That's not true," Ludovico says.

"It is, and you know it."

Ludovico looks at me. I look back at him. He steps away from the doorway—not to say come in, not to say go away, just to make room. Like the space is there if I want it.

I walk through the door.

I don't know yet that I'm not leaving. I don't know that Vincenzo is going to teach me things, or that the woman—Rosalba, her name is Rosalba—is going to put a gold star on the kitchen wall when I get a perfect score on a math test six weeks from now, and that I'm going to have to go into the bathroom and run the water so nobody hears me because I don't know how to be the person who cries about a gold star on a wall.

I don't know any of that yet.

Right now I only know that the floor is warm under my one bare foot, and the house smells like food, and the woman said I was welcome.

For tonight, that's enough.

PRESENT DAY

New York City

THE ESPRESSO HAS BEEN cold for twenty minutes. I'm aware of this in the peripheral way I'm aware of most things—registered, filed, not acted upon because the file in front of me requires my full attention and cold coffee is not a problem with consequences.

The Meridian Waterfront file. Six months of deal preparation, four months of active negotiation under my predecessor, assigned to me three weeks ago when Luca decided the deal required the family's full legal weight. A multibillion-dollar mixed-use Manhattan waterfront development—hotel, commercial, and restaurants. A legitimate acquisition the Lucchese family's transformation under Luca's leadership has been building toward. Lucchese S.r.l. is not only an arms operation. It is a real company with real holdings and real revenue, and this deal is the most significant expansion of the legitimate side of the business in a decade.

I read every document. I know the deal architecture the way I know the family's legal structure—completely. With an eye for the anomalies that matter, and the patience to track them through multiple layers of corporate entity until they resolve into something clear.

I also read the email that arrived this morning, notifying me of the change in opposing counsel.

I read it four times.

Ciccone, C. Colombina Ciccone, managing partner, Ciccone and Associates, Manhattan. The email includes a photograph—a professional headshot, the kind that law firms use for their websites, the kind that's designed to communicate competence and authority. Dark hair. Pale gray eyes. The heart-shaped face I last saw six years ago in a law school hallway in Bologna, with a degree in her hands and a decision in her eyes.

Six years.

I haven't said her name out loud in six years. At odd moments I've thought it, in the spaces between one thing and the next, in the particular silence of 3 a.m. in whichever city I'm in after I handled the operational details and there's nothing left to occupy the part of me that's not the consigliere. I've thought it and set it aside with the discipline of a man who decided and stands by his decisions even when they cost him.

I left her alone because she deserved better than my world of La Cosa Nostra. That was the decision. I stand by it.

I'm also sitting at my desk at 11 p.m. with a cold espresso and an email I've read four times and the specific feeling of a man whose carefully maintained equilibrium has just been disrupted by a professional notification.

I pick up my phone and dial Luca.

Luca answers on the second ring—it's late in Sicily, which means Luca is either working or has been expecting this call, and both are equally possible.

"Flavio."

"The opposing counsel on the Meridian deal. The reassignment. Colombina Ciccone." I pause. "I know her."

A beat. Then Luca says, with the precision of a man who has known me for twenty-three years and reads subtext the way other people read text, "How well."

I glance at the cold espresso. "Well enough."

Another silence. Luca asks, "Do you want me to reassign it?"

The correct answer is yes. The correct answer is: reassign it, keep the deal clean, do not complicate a multibillion-dollar acquisition with personal history. I know this as the consigliere. I give this exact advice to other people in other situations.

"No."

Luca says nothing for a moment. Then he says, "All right." He doesn't ask for an explanation because Luca Lucchese doesn't ask for explanations he already understands. "Be careful with it."

"I'm always careful."

"Yes, which is why I am saying it."

The call ends.

I sit in the penthouse with the Manhattan skyline through the glass and the cold espresso and the professional photograph of a woman who argued with me about property law at 2 a.m. in a library in Bologna six years ago and was right, and I should have told her so then and didn't.

I close the file, reopen it.

The name doesn't change.

Want it. Take it. That is the Lucchese way.

I've wanted Colombina Ciccone since the first night in that library. I let her go because I decided for her, without asking, she deserved better.

She just walked back in across a negotiating table.

I'm not walking away again.

To be continued in the standalone *Taken by the Consigliere: A Dark Mafia Lovers to Enemies to Lovers Romance* (Taken Series: The Lucchese Family Book 3)! Want to be alerted when the full version publishes? Visit CharmaineLouise.com to sign up for my newsletter.

Click the Link Below or Visit books2read.com/u/3yA82L For Your Copy

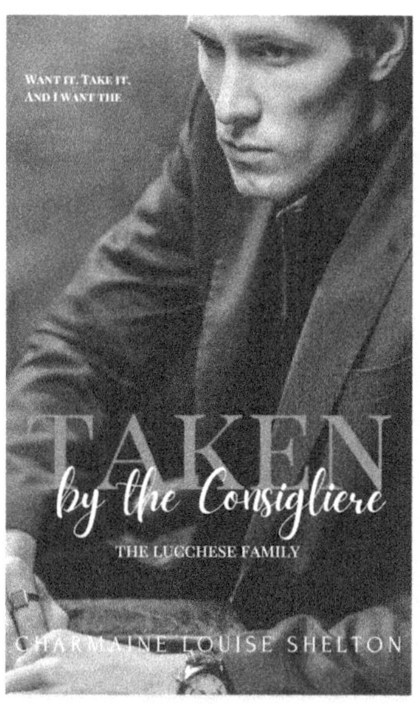

Taken by the Consigliere

STEELE INTERNATIONAL, INC.

A BILLIONAIRES ROMANCE SERIES

Discover My Desires Sebastian & Lola Prequel

(Available Exclusively to Subscribers)

Fulfill My Desires Sebastian & Lola Part I

Heighten My Desires Sebastian & Lola Part II

Gift My Desires Sebastian & Lola First Christmas

Ignite My Desires Roger & Leonie Part I

Stoke My Desires Roger & Leonie Part II

Justify My Desires Roger & Leonie Part III

Deepen My Desires Sebastian & Lola Part III

Capture My Desires Malcolm & Starr Part I

Embrace My Desires Malcolm & Starr Part II

Cherish My Desires Malcolm & Starr Part III

STEELE INTERNATIONAL, INC. - JACKSON CORPORATION

A BILLIONAIRES ROMANCE SERIES CROSSOVER

THE MEN OF STEELE WORLD

Spark My Desires Milly's Men

Incite My Desires Carter & Genevieve

Awaken My Desires Alan & Tabitha

TAKEN SERIES: LUCCHESE FAMILY

Taken by the Enforcer: A Dark Mafia Surprise Baby Romance

Taken by the Capo: A Dark Mafia Revenge Romance

Taken by the Consigliere: A Dark Mafia Lovers to Enemies to Lovers Romance

BILLIONAIRE WOLVES SERIES
WOLF SHIFTER FATED MATES PARANORMAL ROMANCE

MIAMI

Jagger The Awakening
(Available Exclusively to Subscribers)

Jagger The Temptation

Rust The Rejected

Tag The Redemption

<u>Viggo The Obsession</u>

Dylan The Rogue

<u>Billionaire Wolves of Miami — The Complete Collection</u>

NEW YORK

<u>Signy's Mates</u>

<u>Signy Claimed</u>

<u>Signy Forever</u>

<u>Series Playlist</u>

Complete List bit.ly/CharmaineLouiseSheltonBooksList

<u>CharmaineLouiseBooks.com</u>

To read her current works in progress, visit her Ream Stories reamstories.com/charmainelouisebooks.

ABOUT CHARMAINE LOUISE SHELTON

Charmaine Louise Shelton loves a dominant Alpha hero—human, shifter, or vampire—as long as he's a billionaire and sexy as sin! Her romance novels take readers into the heroes' glitzy, glamorous, steamy worlds as they chase after independent women who unexpectedly capture their hearts.

Want to experience some more? Follow her on social media on your favorite channels below. Read her current works in progress at her Ream Stories bit.ly/Charmaine LouiseBooksCoterie. Join her newsletter for the latest updates, releases, and more bit.ly/CLBooksJoin Newsletter.

Find her at:
CharmaineLouiseBooks.com

Fulfill Your Desires.

bookbub.com/authors/charmaine-louise-shelton

tiktok.com/@authorcharmainelouise

youtube.com/@charmainelouisebooks

facebook.com/CharmaineLouiseBooks

instagram.com/charmainelouisebooks

goodreads.com/charmainelouisebooks

DEDICATION

*To my awesome and dedicated beta readers and ARC Team,
my amazing author friends, and this incredible community for
their support.*

*And most of all to you, my loyal readers who love these couples
as much as I do.*

Thank you!

Fulfill Your Desires.

xoxo
Charmaine Louise Shelton